TEMPLE OF THE DAWN

When Lexa took a job in Thailand as
nanny to little six-year-old Alacho
Mansell she soon lost her heart to her
small charge. But she also came to love
the child's father, Paul—a man whose
heart belonged, as it always would, to
his beautiful dead wife Sally . . .

TEMPLE OF THE DAWN

BY

ANNE HAMPSON

MILLS & BOON LIMITED
17–19 FOLEY STREET
LONDON W1A 1DR

First published 1979
Australian copyright 1979
Philippine copyright 1979
This edition 1979

© Anne Hampson 1979

ISBN 0 263 73147 2

Set in Linotype Times 10 on 11½ pt.

Made and printed in Great Britain by
Richard Clay (The Chaucer Press), Ltd., Bungay, Suffolk

CHAPTER ONE

A SHIMMERING blue haze hung over the Don Muang Airport as the great jet swung down to touch the runway.
Lexa felt the first gentle bump and thought with a sudden frown that she should not be here at all, thousands of
miles from the tiny Shropshire village where she was
perfectly happy in her job, and with life generally.

It had all begun with the appearance at the school of
the formidable Paul Mansell who had brought his six-
year-old daughter to be a temporary pupil in Lexa's class
of second-year infants.

His severity with the child, his total indifference to the
love she obviously wanted to give him, had angered Lexa
from the first; her dislike grew and after only the third
meeting she actually believed she hated him. And it had
nothing to do with the terrible scar on his otherwise handsome face, a scar running from the right ear down to his
chin, obviously the result of a ghastly burn. No, it certainly was not the scar that put her off him; it was his
manner with the child, and also his manner with herself.
For he treated her as an inferior, someone whose func-
tion it was to do him a service, and from whom he
expected good service. His voice, though abrupt, was
tempered by the soft Irish brogue that came through its
innate hardness.

'Granny was Irish,' Alacho had said, 'and I'm named
after her. Do you like my name?'

'It's very pretty,' replied Lexa, then added, 'Your
daddy's father wasn't Irish, though?' She was thinking

5

of his name, which was in no way Irish.

'He was English; but he's dead now as well as Granny. Mummy's dead too. I don't remember her because I was only one when she died.'

The child had seemed so utterly lost and lonely that Lexa, who had hitherto determinedly resolved never to favour one child more than another, found herself pampering her a little, giving her the occasional hug, talking to her in the playground, slipping an arm about her tiny waist. She tried to glean some information about her background, but learned very little. All she did learn was that the father had once lived in England but was now permanently residing in Thailand, that 'Land of Smiles' whose long southern peninsula was washed on one side by the South China Sea and on the other by the warm waters of the Indian Ocean.

'I want to see you, Miss Duke,' the Headmistress had said one morning in Assembly. 'Come to my room at half-past ten, as soon as the children have gone out to play.'

Lexa, who had been teaching for four years, was at the age of twenty-five fairly confident of her ability in her chosen profession, so the summons held no fears for her; she knew instinctively that Miss Saunders had no complaints to grumble about. Lexa adored young children and often her colleagues asked why she didn't get married and have a family of her own. She had Joe, they said, and he was 'nice'.

Yes, she had Joe, and yes, he was nice. But there was a stolid quality about him that seemed to override any emotion he might otherwise have exhibited. Quiet as Lexa was, with no excitement in her life, she knew instinctively that she wanted something very different from marriage from what Joe was able to give. And so they remained friends, going out together now and then, playing tennis, swimming. Both were satisfied with the relationship and each was prepared for the time when the inevitable parting would occur.

'You're going to be very surprised by what I have to tell you,' Miss Saunders had said when, at the appointed time, Lexa had gone to her room. 'Sit down and I'll give you the message.' The telephone had just rung and she picked up the receiver, staring at Lexa while she listened to the young mother at the other end of the line, giving an explanation as to why Jimmy could not attend school that day.

Miss Saunders, forty-five and greying rapidly, had long since given up hope of attracting a man. She was happy in her work and saw no hardship in continuing until she retired at the age of sixty. But she had often wished she had the youth and looks of her youngest teacher, the girl who had come to her straight from college, and who was settled and happy, with a flat in the village—well, not a flat really, but part of a house owned by a couple who, retired and living on their pensions, had decided to let part of the house to a 'single lady with sober habits: a non-smoker, and preferably over thirty'. Lexa had seen the advertisement on the same day she had been interviewed for the post. Although only twenty-one at the time, she had made a favourable enough impression on Mr and Mrs Newland for them to accept her as a tenant. She had been there ever since, had become part of the village life. She was totally unaware of what was to be offered, mused Miss Saunders, still staring at her, taking in the delicate lines and contours of her face, the sweet young mouth, wide, compassionate. Her hair was pale gold sprinkled with darker threads here and there—copper, almost, so attractive. It was long, down to her shoul-

ders where the ends turned up naturally . . . a lovely frame
for a beautiful face. . . .

Sensing her superior's interest, Lexa glanced towards
her, a half-enquiring look in her large, widely-spaced
violet-blue eyes. The Head smiled, replaced the receiver
and sat down on the opposite side of the desk.

'Alacho's father is returning to Thailand,' she said
without preamble, 'and he wants to take you with him.'

'Take——' Lexa stared uncomprehendingly. 'I don't
know what you mean, Miss Saunders?'

The smile broadened, yet there was a sigh in the words
which came next.

'He wants a nanny for his daughter. Apparently that's
the main reason why he came over for this visit, although
he was visiting friends around these parts, hence the
reason for renting the Masons' holiday cottage for three
months. He had a long talk with me yesterday afternoon
after you'd gone home.' A pause and the intake of a
breath to accompany a slight frown. 'I suppose I'm
wanting you to refuse, while at the same time very conscious of the opportunity offered in this post. The salary
he's offering is incredible——' She mentioned it, watching Lexa's eyes widen to their fullest extent. 'Also, there's
the chance of seeing something of the other side of the
world, of living in luxury.' She stopped, waiting, but
Lexa was too taken aback to offer any response at this
moment. 'He's been advertising and apparently the
numerous applicants have all been rejected. He's a difficult man to please; that much I quickly gathered. I
should imagine he'd be a hard and exacting employer,
but I feel you could manage to hold your own with him.
I'm speaking from four years' experience,' she added
with a faint curve of her lips. Lexa coloured slightly,
aware that the Head was thinking of the one or two

tussles she had had with unpleasant mothers who had nothing good to say either for the school or the teachers. One always got them, and it was a clever teacher who could manage to unruffle these mothers while at the same time winning a victory over them.

'My Vicky is *not* playing out in the cold!'

'Our girlie's not used to little boys. I don't want her sitting near them, or playing in the Wendy house with them.'

'Susan's been telling me that they were playing mothers and fathers! Her daddy and I were shocked to hear her say she was having a baby!'

Lexa, feeling she had been born with more genes for diplomacy and tact than most of the people she knew, had her little scraps with these mothers, but in the end she always convinced them that they were wrong and she was right. The crisp autumn air was *good* for Vicky, and anyway, wouldn't she feel out of it, left alone in the classroom? Mary *ought* to have the company of little boys, because she was unusually shy and needed bringing out.

And so it had gone on, with Miss Saunders allowing the mothers to go along and see Lexa, convinced that the girl would send them away not only pacified but happy.

'You're very quiet, Miss Duke.' The Headmistress's voice interrupted Lexa's reverie and she looked at her across the wide, well-worn desk top.

'You say I could manage to hold my own with Mr Mansell——' Lexa shook her head, a frown knitting her brows, shading her eyes. 'I dislike him intensely, Miss Saunders, and I had an idea that you did too, but apparently you don't?'

A small silence followed and then,

'I've learned a bit about him,' Miss Saunders said, and her face had a brooding expression almost as if she were in deep sympathy with the man. 'I've just said that he's here visiting friends. Well, I was at a meeting a couple of weeks ago and somehow I got into conversation with a teacher who happened to be a friend of the daughter of one of these friends of his.' She paused a moment. 'To cut a long story short, he got that scar in trying to save his wife from a burning building—the house in which they lived. But he'd used up precious time in getting Alacho out first. She was in the nursery on the ground floor, with her nanny. The nanny grabbed him as he was going upstairs to his wife and in her frenzy she wouldn't let go of him until he had gone in to the baby and brought her out. Well, when he got his wife out she was too far gone—overcome with smoke and burns. She died in his arms.'

'How terrible! But the nanny? Why didn't she get the baby out herself? Apparently she was capable of doing so?'

'She panicked, totally. Had no idea what she was saying or doing——' Miss Saunders shrugged her shoulders, going on to say that under circumstances such as those, with the house blazing from ground floor to roof, people did act irrationally, overcome with fear and panic to the point where clear thought and common sense deserted them altogether.

'So that's why he has no love for his daughter....' Lexa spoke to herself, all her pity going out to the child. She still could not understand why her father should adopt the attitude he had. True, the loss of his wife was a tragedy, but that was no excuse for depriving his little daughter of love.

'He was madly in love with his wife and has never got over her death. He was in business in Cheshire at the time, but his childhood had been spent in Thailand where his father owned several hotels. These were left to his son, who went over about every two years, just to talk to the managers. When the tragedy occurred he decided to leave England and live in Thailand——' Again the Headmistress shrugged. 'That's about all. He has no idea that we know anything more about him than what he's told us himself—with perhaps the scraps of information you've gleaned from Alacho. So if you do take the job you'll have to be careful.'

Even before she stopped speaking Lexa was shaking her head.

'I'm happy here, Miss Saunders, and I want to stay. It was kind of you to give me the opportunity of the money and the travel, but I won't take it.' She got up. 'Is there anything else?' she asked politely and with a smile. Miss Saunders was, strangely enough, frowning, instead of being relieved, as Lexa expected.

'You haven't given it any thought, Miss Duke. Don't make a decision yet. Sleep on it for one night at least. And consider the child. She's happy with you—happier, I imagine, than she has been for a very long time.'

Lexa nodded mechanically, recalling what the child had told her about the Thai nanny she had had at first. The girl had married later and from then on there had been a succession of English nannies, brought over by her father without his having seen them personally. They had obviously not been satisfactory, or perhaps they hadn't been able to settle in a strange country where Buddhism was the main religion. Whatever the reason, Paul Mansell had resolved never again to risk engaging another nanny by post, as it were, but had decided to come over to England, combining a holiday with the serious business of finding a suitable person to look after his child.

And it was the child herself who finally persuaded

Lexa to accept the post. She pleaded, staring up mistily at Lexa with her big brown eyes, pleading eyes that matched the quivering entreaties that left the little girl's lips.

'I want you, Miss Duke—only—only y-you and not any other lady—to—to look after me.'

The father, stern, devoid of emotion, the scar livid against a throat where a nerve pulsated, watched Lexa's changing expression and eventually turned away. She had weakened; help had come from her Headmistress whose feelings, though mixed, for certainly she would feel Lexa's loss acutely, were both with the man and his daughter. At present, she was more in sympathy with Paul Mansell than Lexa, who still disliked him in spite of what he had suffered, but Miss Saunders felt sure that with time Lexa would come to feel differently towards the man.

The bluish mist began to disperse immediately the airport was left behind. A chauffeur-driven car had met Lexa; her luggage, after going through Customs with the minimum of fuss, was stowed away in the huge boot and she was in the car, her mind not at all calm or even clear. She was in a sort of vacuum, neither in one place nor another, like not having a home, or people, or any kind of stability.

And, come to think of it, it was exactly like that! No home or people ... just no one of her own or anything remotely familiar.

A rather frightening thought, and she decided it was better to attempt to forget it and concentrate on what was passing as the car sped smoothly on its way, covering the twenty-four kilometres between the airport and the city of Bangkok where she was to be met by her em-

ployer at the Ayudhya Palace Hotel, one of the several
which he owned in the capital. His home—when he could
get to it—was on the delightful coral island of Koh Kham
where, Alacho had said, the sand was silver and soft as
talcum powder, where the house in which they lived was
set amidst coconut palms and fragrant frangipani and
hibiscus trees. There was a fountain and swimming-pool,
shady verandahs and a courtyard, a private beach and
jetty, where her daddy's yacht was moored.

'But he can't come home much,' Alacho had added,
shadows in her eyes suddenly, 'because he's too busy at
the hotels.'

The road was good, the huge car a dream of perfection. Lexa, though still dazed and wondering, managed
to look out. The Suriwong Road where the shops seemed
to be bursting with glorious Thai silk or brocade dolls
or jewellery to set any woman's eyes popping out of her
head. A couple of babies, looking like twins, were eating
tropical fruit under the shade of a tree; a parchment-
faced man watched them—their grandfather, probably.
The car came on to the New Road, which was flanked
with administrative buildings. And then the chauffeur
slowed down, coming to a halt finally before the colonial-
style façade of one of Bangkok's most opulent hotels, the
Ayudhya Palace in Oriental Avenue by the Chao Phya
River.

Lexa gasped at the splendour as she entered a lobby
that was every bit elegantly Thai, sumptuously carpeted;
decorated walls in gold leaf, mirrors and chandeliers—
beauty and luxury everywhere.

'You will want your luggage, I believe.' The chauffeur,
a smiling Thai, had obviously been given instructions
beforehand.

Lexa was staring around when she spotted Paul Man-

sell striding towards her, his tall, sinewed frame clad
in white linen, immaculate, breathtakingly attractive, and
she caught her breath, amazed that she should be feeling anything other than distaste for the inevitable interview that was about to follow the meeting. No smile
affected the severity of his features, no hint of welcome
changed the chill hardness of his deep-set, steely-grey
eyes. She glanced at his hair, noticing the threads of
grey at the temples. She pondered his age for an instant
and decided he was at least thirty-five. And as his hand
was extended towards her she saw for the first time that
it carried a slight scar close to the wrist. She shuddered,
faintly annoyed that she should be thinking of that terrible experience he had gone through, entering a burning
building to bring out the wife he loved and whose death
had almost broken him.

'You had a pleasant, uneventful flight?' were his first
words after a brief and impersonal greeting.

'Fairly pleasant for the most part,' she answered. 'But
not altogether uneventful. We ran into a storm.'

He shrugged, and she realised that what to her had
been a frightening experience would be nothing at all
to him.

Perhaps, she thought, he would be glad to die.

'You had to work out your full two months' notice,'
he said. 'I had hopes that you wouldn't be forced to do
so.'

'Miss Saunders would have let me go, but the Educa-
tion Authority were firm that I should work my full
notice. How is Alacho, Mr Mansell? Is she well, and
happy?'

He looked down at Lexa from his great height, and
his expression was faintly contemptuous, as if he thought
nothing of her for putting a question to which she already knew the answer.

'She certainly isn't happy. I'm sure you know full well just how much you mean to her where happiness is concerned. She loves you as she has never loved anyone before.'

No bitterness in the tone. It struck Lexa—not without pain and regret—that Paul Mansell cared not one jot whether his daughter loved him or not.

'She'll be happy now, though? You've told her I'm coming today?'

He shook his head in silence and walked away, indicating with a flick of his hand that she should follow. At the desk she was greeted with, '*Sawadee!*'—a welcome to the 'Land of Smiles'. She was told the number of her room, then taken to it by a uniformed porter, buff-skinned and smiling, his jet black hair short and gleaming as if it had been polished. Paul Mansell had told her to meet him in the lounge on what he called the Lotus Deck, at one o'clock, which was in half an hour's time. They would have a chat over lunch, he had ended abruptly before, having satisfied himself that she was being looked after, he strode away.

The room to which she was shown was breathtakingly lovely, with typical Thai decor—carpets in bedroom and sitting-room sumptuous, like those in the great lobby downstairs. The bathroom had both bath and shower, and was in a most delicate shade of green, with one entire wall covered with a mirror.

How long would she be here? Lexa wondered, a sigh on her lips. She felt desperately alone and unhappy, yet even if she had been given the choice again she could not imagine herself acting any differently.

After a shower and change of dress she felt rather better in spirits. A look in the mirror provided a further booster, because she saw a slender wand of a girl in crisp copper-rose linen, the dress sleeveless and low at the neck; she saw hair gleaming from the vigorous brushing she had given it, saw limpid blue eyes beneath curving brows, a wide forehead, and the trace of blue veins at her temples, showing through the delicate transparency of her skin. Her hands were small, dainty, with almond-shaped nails polished but not varnished. She looked younger than her years, she mused, and for no reason at all found herself reflecting on the age she had given to her employer and wondering if the experience he had gone through had made *him* appear *older* than his years.

Strangely she could not grasp the fact that he was her employer. He was a man apart, remote not only from her and his child but from everyone around him. On his visits to the school he had been so distant that she had never been able to fathom the reason for his coming at all. He had of course—she now realised—been weighing her up, assessing her worth as a nanny for his child. Yes, there had been a reason for those visits, but although he had her under observation he had never by so much as the flicker of an eyelid given Lexa an inkling that he was interested in her as an employee.

She saw him immediately she entered the lounge. He rose from the chair on which he was sitting, a glass on the small table in front of him. The lounge had one side entirely open, to the view of a swiming-pool shaded by palms and frangipani trees and with low bushes here and there—ylang-ylang shrubs whose scented flowers with greenish-yellow petals had given it the name of Perfume Tree; the allamandas, slender climbers whose flowers were of mauve or purple, very different from the yellow ones Lexa had seen on her way from the airport. There were bushes of the lipstick plant, clusters of wax begonias and China asters, and the dainty cosmos whose white and orange and purple flowers bloomed throughout the year.

'Right on time, Miss Duke.' Paul Mansell's tone was brusque but, as before, Lexa noticed the softness of the Irish brogue coming through. It was most attractive, something that was at total variance with the rest of him, yet something he could never lose. It was a pity that Alacho did not have it, thought Lexa, taking the chair he offered to her.

He asked what she was drinking and ordered it for her.

'You found everything to your liking?' he said when the waiter had gone.

Lexa nodded, wanting to talk, to hear him telling her what was expected of her. She wanted to know about Alacho, and how she was going on.

'You asked if Alacho was happy now,' he said as if guessing at her impatience. 'As a matter of fact, I haven't told her you're coming.'

'Not told her?' Lexa blinked at him. 'But surely you *should* have done? I mean,' she hastened to add on seeing the sudden frown appear on his brow, 'I'd have thought you would want to tell her, to reassure her.'

He looked directly at her.

'Right up to the moment of seeing you, Miss Duke, I had no faith in your promise to take on the job.'

'Mr Mansell,' returned Lexa with slow emphasis, 'I never break a promise. Even if I'd changed my mind I'd still have come, temporarily, until you were able to find someone else.'

'Then accept my apology.' He glanced away, to seek the waiter. The apology meant nothing, decided Lexa, disliking him more than ever. Why couldn't he smile, make her feel welcome? True, he was desperately unhappy, but surely he realised that one cannot live with the dead? Surely he wasn't going to let the memory of his dead wife haunt him till the end of his days? But sharp on these thoughts came the admission that one had to experience a sorrow personally to know what the reaction was. She herself had lost her parents, but not by death. Her father had run off with someone else when Lexa was only four years old; and when she was starting at college, a resident, her mother confessed that she had had someone else for several years and that she now felt free to live her own life. She had got married within three months of Lexa's entering the college and was now living with her husband in South America. Lexa had never visited them but she had written a lot at first. Her mother, though, often failed to answer and at last their link was merely by an odd letter during the year and cards and presents for birthdays and Christmas.

With Lexa, her job was all-absorbing, and this, combined with her part in the village activities, gave her all she wanted from life at present. As was to be expected, she had her visions of a future with a husband and children, a pretty home—not luxurious, probably, but a little castle for all that, a stronghold founded on love and trust and friendship. That she was unlikely to meet her dream man in the village had long since come right home to her, but she was a fatalist and as such believed that she would meet him one day—and she believed too that she would realise she had met him the very moment of setting her eyes upon him. Love at first sight. Oh, yes, she really did believe she would know her dream man instantly. And he would know her; they both would read love in their first look into one another's eyes.

She had been staring at the couple over in a corner, holding hands, and now and then kissing lightly. But she turned her golden head as she heard Paul Mansell say,

'You'll be staying here for the next couple of days, Miss Duke, as I can't spare the time to take you to Koh Kham until Friday. I shall then be able to have the week-end at home.'

'Alacho ... she's being looked after?' It was a silly question, she knew, even before he had raised his eyebrows in a gesture of faint contempt.

'I'd scarcely leave my daughter without making sure she was looked after. She's in the charge of one of the maids.'

'I'm sorry; I didn't think.' In spite of the colour that came to her cheeks there was a calm, demure charm about her face that seemed suddenly to arrest his attention. She was naturally embarrassed by the snub and yet able to don a veneer of composure. 'I really meant that I ought to be with her, doing the job I came here to do.'

'You haven't been a nanny before?'

'No, I've been teaching since I left college.'

'You chose the youngest children. Obviously you could have taught older ones, had you wanted to?'

She nodded.

'Yes; but the little ones are more interesting to me. They're so helpless when they first come to school. I took the reception class at first,' she went on to explain. 'They'd never been away from their mothers before— well, not for any length of time. Often they cry, and sometimes try to run home. It's pathetic——' She broke off, biting her lip, feeling silly and sentimental because her eyes were far too bright and her voice had quivered with emotion. 'They're still babies at five,' she added finally.

'And at six?'

'They can be very grown up. It's amazing what that first year at school does for them.'

'I find that Alacho doesn't grow up at all.' Hard the

tone, implacable. Undoubtedly he had no understanding of children and their needs. On impulse Lexa said, looking straight into his eyes,

'Love and security are the two essentials to a child's development, Mr Mansell. Deny it those and you retard its healthy growth.'

The steely eyes were suddenly sharpened to glittering points.

'You're accusing me of neglect,' he said in a very soft tone of voice.

Lexa shuddered, wishing she were somewhere else—outside in the sunshine, or back at school. No, not back at school. She was needed here and no matter what she had to endure from the father she meant to do all she could for the child.

'It isn't my place to criticise,' she answered.

'But you have your own private opinions?'

'Please don't embarrass me,' she begged, giving an indrawn breath of relief as she saw the waiter appear with the drinks.

'You're honest,' said Paul when the man had gone, 'and I admire honesty. I hope you will always be honest with me, remembering what I just said about admiring honesty. If ever there's anything that doesn't fit in with your ideas of bringing up my daughter then let me know. Understand?'

'Of course, Mr Mansell. I'm to have a free hand, then?'

'So far. But I too shall have some say. I believe in firmness from an early age. Any child will play up if he or she thinks for one moment such behaviour is going to get them what they want. Alacho has never had any of her own way, and I want you to understand that she never will have her own way.'

Appalled, Lexa could only stare for several seconds,

watching him as he picked up his glass and put it to his mouth.

'Mr Mansell,' she managed at length, 'how on earth is Alacho to develop normally if she is never allowed to do what *she* wants to do. Only puppets respond indefinitely to string-pulling.' She was angry by now and it showed. She could not conceive of being successful in her job of nanny if she was expected to suppress all the child's natural tendencies. 'You never intimated, in the interview we had, that I was to crush her personality.' Strong words, but Lexa wanted to impress him forcibly with what she was saying. He too was angry, his eyes glinting more coldly than ever.

'There's a difference between crushing her personality and allowing her to get out of hand,' he snapped. Lexa said nothing and after a moment he added, 'Let's not go into this any further. Lunch is ordered for us in the Mandarin Grill——' He glanced at his wristwatch. 'It's time we were going in.'

She drank up, uncomfortably aware that he watched her impatiently, his own glass having been emptied several minutes ago. She rose at last, and was taken across the wide pool patio to an entrance that was heavily carved with strange figures, some beautiful, some positively ugly. But the Mandarin Grill was superb, with candles lit even at this time of day. Situated on the top floor, it had a panoramic view of the busy river with its numerous sampans drifting along, some piled high with vegetables. The city came into the same picture, a fairyland of golden pinnacles and elaborately-decorated roofs, dazzlingly coloured and gleaming in the sunshine. Ornate statues were everywhere, and the most delicate carvings—all on temples, of which there were no less than three hundred in the city of Bangkok alone ... three hundred Buddhist temples....

'It's—beautiful!' Lexa exclaimed enthusiastically. 'You know, Mr Mansell, one reads of these cities of the world, and it does seem that the picture is fairly clear in one's mind, but it's only when one visits the place that one realises just how lacking one's imagination is.' She was smiling in her enthusiasm, forgetting her dislike of the man who was her companion. He was someone to talk to, and she asked about the temples, seeking his advice as to which of them she ought to visit. He told her of the Emerald Buddha, housed in the temple called Wat Phra Keo.

'It's in the grounds of the Grand Palace,' he added when they were seated, at a table for two in a secluded corner by the window. 'You'll find a white castellated wall enclosing a vast compound with a whole cluster of Thai-style buildings, and the Temple of the Emerald Buddha is the most impressive of them all. This temple is in fact the private temple of the King and Queen of Thailand.' He went on to warn her that she must dress in a conservative manner. 'No shorts or scanty tops; and you can't take a camera into the temple.'

Lexa listened avidly as, after ordering, he went on to describe other temples which she ought to see. There was Wat Sakret, a man-made mountain surmounted by a magnificent gold pagoda—or *chedi,* as it was called—which housed the relics of the Lord Buddha. There was the Temple of the Golden Buddha, the Temple of the Dawn, and so many others that it would be impossible for her to see them all.

'I suppose,' she was saying later, when they had lunched on grilled lobster Bayonnaise washed down with a dry white wine, 'I shall be on the island most of the time? You don't bring Alacho here, I suppose?'

'I've brought her on three or four occasions—for one reason or another. I can't remember,' he added indifferently. 'Perhaps her nanny was ill, or something. However, I shan't have any problems now that you are here.'

The way he said that brought a warmth to Lexa in spite of there being neither friendliness nor emotion in the words. She smiled, then wished she hadn't, since there was not even the movement of a muscle in response. Strange, unfathomable man! She recalled him declaring he would have some say in the way Alacho was brought up, but she now strongly suspected he had not meant a word of it. He was indifferent, totally so, and Lexa believed the words were spoken merely as a warning to her not to spoil the child. As for what he had said about Alacho not growing up—well, Lexa had seen a great change in her while she was at school, and the change would continue. She was satisfied that progress would be made, and could only hope she was correct in her assumption that Paul had no intention of interfering in the way she would be handling his daughter.

CHAPTER TWO

IT was the beginning of April, and the so-called cool season had ended about a month ago. Now was the hot season, but on the tiny island of Koh Kham cool breezes tempered the excessive heat and Lexa found no difficulty in giving Alacho her lessons, nor in the child taking in what she was taught. The afternoons were taken up with swimming in the pool or in the sea, with rambles through rich forest land where orchids dripped colour from every tree. Alacho was happy and her attitude showed it in every way. An intelligent child, she seemed to take an interest in everything around her. Dolls and toys did not interest her, though; she would rather play with her dog, Pango, or talk with Lexa. Often she was with the Thai servants with whom she was popular and always had been.

They spoke English fluently, so there were no problems either for the child or her nanny. Lexa had fitted in far more easily than she had expected; she had been here over a month and not once had her employer interfered with the way she was teaching his daughter. He had been home for two week-ends in the four and was due home again on Friday evening. Even when he was home Lexa saw little of him, but on one occasion he had swum in the sea with her and Alacho, and he and Lexa had sat on the soft warm sands afterwards, talking casually as they watched Alacho playing with another little girl, the daughter of visitors to one of Paul's neighbours.

Lexa had been strangely affected by his presence on

that particular day, for he seemed less distant, more human. But he never smiled, never showed any sense of humour at all. He dined alone, in the large saloon which was never otherwise used. From the servants Lexa learned that he never entertained, never had a visitor even.

What a lonely life for a man still comparatively young! Once again Lexa found herself wondering if he intended grieving for his wife for the rest of his days.

Alacho was now calling her Auntie Lexa, having decided that Miss Duke did not sound at all friendly.

'You're not a schoolteacher any more,' she went on to add unnecessarily, 'so I shouldn't have to call you Miss Duke, should I?' A rather mischievous grin accompanied the words and Lexa, by now very used to the change in Alacho, grinned in response and agreed that as she was no longer a schoolteacher it was all right for her to be called auntie. However, when Paul heard it, on the Friday evening, he frowned disapprovingly and asked in curt and arrogant tones why Lexa had allowed such familiarity.

'I don't call it familiarity,' she returned, angry because his displeasure hurt in some absurd way that caused resentment to rise within her. Granted, his displeasure ought to cause some anxiety, but certainly not hurt. 'After all, I shall be here a long time and Alacho can't keep on called me Miss Duke.'

'Why not?'

'Well. . . .' Lexa had no answer, which only increased her anger. The brevity of his question was in itself a snub, a sign of the arrogance which she had early observed to be an innate part of him. 'I'd rather she called me auntie,' ended Lexa lamely, turning from the disconcerting scrutiny of those steely grey eyes.

'I would rather she didn't.' Even the soft burr could not take the cold authority from his voice. 'You're no relation, just an employee, and therefore such familiarity is not to be considered.'

Lexa swallowed, but said nothing. The man was insufferable! She wished he would not come home at all, but stay in Bangkok where he seemed far happier—if the man *could* be happy!

Alacho had eventually to be told she was not allowed to call Lexa auntie, and to Lexa's utter surprise the child's eyes blazed and she raced into the room where her father was sitting, listening to records. Her small fists were clenched and her face was white as she cried,

'I'm calling her auntie, so there, Daddy! I love her and I want her for my auntie. She loves me, and you don't, so I don't love you any more——!'

'Alacho!' Lexa had come after her, but not swiftly enough. She grasped her hand and tugged her round. Her father rose slowly to his feet, tall, overpowering, frightening. The scar was livid, that nerve pulsating as it had once before, but now the movement was the result of anger—no, fury, white-hot and terrible.

'You don't love me, Alacho?' So soft the tone, so filled with hidden hatred. 'But you love Miss Duke?'

'Yes. . . .' Alacho's voice faltered; she was afraid of her father, terrified of his anger, quiet though it was. 'I w-want her for—for m-my auntie——' The voice broke in a strangled cry as her other wrist was gripped. Lexa let go of the one she held—swiftly let go because she knew what was about to happen. Alacho was swung across her father's knee, but even before one blow was struck Lexa was there, fighting him, pulling her charge away, but gently. Paul, who had rested one foot on the low chair that happened to be handy, almost over-

balanced when Lexa's body catapulted into his, and
he had to release his hold upon his daughter. His fury
grew to white-hot proportions and even Lexa was frightened, her heart pounding against her ribs, her nerves
all awry.

Alacho was crying quietly, her face hidden in Lexa's
skirt. Silence reigned otherwise in the room, for the
record had ended and the machine had switched itself
off. Paul and Lexa faced one another across the distance
separating them, fury and hatred in his eyes, contempt
in hers.

'Take her away,' he snarled. 'Take her out of my
sight—and keep her out of it!'

Pulse racing and heart thumping, Lexa did as he
ordered, marvelling that she could manage to use her
legs, since they felt too weak to carry her trembling
body. What a scene! And all her fault for not guessing
that Alacho might react in this way. It wasn't as if she
was ignorant of the child's temper; she had witnessed it
several times at school, and on a couple of occasions
since. She was headstrong, yet affectionate, wilful and
at the same time so very lovable. A strange mixture,
and Lexa felt that it was no wonder, with a father like
hers, that she had vices. Perhaps she had inherited her
virtues from her mother.

'I'm sorry, Auntie Lexa,' wept the child when they
were in the nursery, a beautiful room on the first floor
of the villa, its view to the sea, with the glorious garden
and grounds in between. A verandah ran the whole
length of one wall, a verandah dripping with exotic
flowers, and where pretty garden chairs were set round
an equally pretty little table. The room itself was fur-
nished with every luxurious fitting imaginable. Yes,
Alacho had everything except love.

'Take her away. Take her out of my sight—and keep her out of it.'

God, would she ever be able to get such words out of her mind! Lexa hugged the child, bending down to press her face to one tear-drenched, burning cheek. Take her away. . . . His little daughter, his own flesh and blood!

'I wish it was possible, you fiend! I wish with all my heart I had the right to take her from you!' She spoke silently, but her whole body trembled with the intensity of her fury.

'Don't cry, my darling. Daddy didn't mean it.'

'He did! He's said things like that before! He hates me, and when I'm big enough I'll run away!' Renewed weeping; it went right through Lexa and she silently cursed Paul Mansell for his cruelty.

'Alacho dear, please stop crying. You're making me unhappy too.' And it was the truth; Lexa's eyes were filled with tears, her heart dragged down with pain. 'It's still early afternoon. Shall we go on to the beach?' It was Saturday; Lexa hoped that Paul would leave to-morrow and not stay on till Monday morning, as he had done last week-end. How was he feeling? Was he ashamed of his conduct? she wondered, spitefully wishing she could bring him to the same depths of misery as those to which he had brought his innocent little daughter.

'I don't w-want t-to go—any-anywhere——' Great sobs choked the words, which were muffled anyway, because Alacho's face was buried in Lexa's skirt.

'We'll both feel better for being outside, love. Come with me. I very much want to walk on the beach.'

After a while the sobs became less frequent, then died altogether. Alacho consented to going out, but the stroll on the beach was a silent one, for both of them were still very unhappy. Lexa wondered what was the wisest thing to do. Perhaps to ignore it would be best, she was thinking one moment, while the next found her determined to seek Paul out that evening after Alacho was in bed and have a verbal battle with him. Would he send her away, though? She rather believed she would be kept on. He had come to depend on her; and in any case, there was no one to take her place.

Yes, she was sure her position was strong enough for a protest to do little harm, and when the child was tucked up in bed, and drowsy after being read to for twenty minutes, Lexa went to the sitting-room and knocked on the door. There was no answer and she undid the catch and slid the door inwards. Paul was sitting there, on a narrow window seat, his head in his hands. Withdrawing swiftly, Lexa pulled the door to, then knocked again, more loudly this time. Pity rose unbidden, pity for him there alone, his head in his hands. . . . So unhappy, so desperately sunk in grief.

'Come in.' The voice was so low she hardly heard it.

'I'd like to speak to you, Mr Mansell,' she said, walking in and pushing the door to behind her. 'It's about Alacho—but you'll guess that.' She advanced slowly, to where he was now standing, his back to the window. Darkness outside caused shadows to veil his face so that it appeared almost evil, with the terrible scar seeming to be raised up, and that nerve pulsating, the nerve he seemed unable to control. Her eyes fell to his hand, resting on the back of a chair. The scar was infinitesimal compared with the one on his face, but it, too, was red and angry at this moment. 'May I sit down?'

'Of course.' His abrupt gesture indicated the sofa, but she chose a chair. 'What is it you want? You're giving me your notice?'

'Do you really believe I'm made of that kind of stuff, Mr Mansell?' she enquired tautly.

'It would be understandable if you wanted to leave.' He spoke roughly, but all the former anger was quenched —probably by the misery which now obviously engulfed him.

'I shall never willingly desert Alacho. She needs me. She has no one else to love, or to love her.'

He did not flinch, as Lexa had hoped he would. As usual, he seemed unable to show any kind of emotion where his child was concerned. For a moment Lexa toyed with the idea of telling him that she knew why he was like this with Alacho, but decided against it. Miss Saunders had told it in confidence, but Lexa wished she hadn't, for it seemed that complete honesty on both sides was the only way to resolve the situation that was affecting them all.

'You're becoming possessive about her,' he said.

'I'm not, but would it matter at all to you if I was?'

The grey eyes kindled.

'You're being very blunt, Miss Duke. I was told by your headmistres that you were adept at using tact. I find you quite the reverse.'

'Tact won't help, Mr Mansell, but plain speaking will. Tell me, please, why you're like this with your dear little girl?'

'Dear little girl. . . .' Soft the tone, and heartbreakingly bitter. It was easy to guess at his thoughts as he brooded there, his mouth moving spasmodically, his hand clenched at his side. Alacho, his dear little girl, was responsible, indirectly it was true, for his inability to save his wife from a terrible death. He spoke, fiercely, but to himself, his grey eyes staring vacantly, staring directly into Lexa's but without seeing her at all. 'Do you know that when

anyone is burned to death the heart and brain go last?'
Lexa shuddered, shaking her head as if to throw off
the picture produced by her imagination. 'So you can
realise what a person suffers, Miss Duke. *The heart and
brain live on, through it all—until the end——*' His voice
was raised in agony, the voice of a man on the borders
of madness. Perspiration began to pour from his brow
and with a vicious swipe he removed it, only to make
way for more. His eyes, no longer hard, no longer fixed
on Lexa's face, were moist ... *moist*!

Lexa's heart twisted within her, and wept for him.
The very awareness that his misery went so deep that
it could bring him to the point of tears sent a great flood
of compassion through her body and mind, but there was
something else even stronger, something that propelled
her to action, and she ran to him and flung her arms
about his waist. It was a primitive, impulsive gesture
which seemed not to surprise him. He bent his head, and
without being consciously aware of it she brought it to her
breast, holding it there while her other hand came forward to stroke his face where the scar shone red, blood-
red. Long moments passed in silence before he moved,
lifting a dazed and haggard face, his lips convulsed as he
tried in vain to articulate words. Several more seconds
elapsed before at last he did manage to speak, drawing
away as he said,

'I'm sorry.' His voice, abrupt and cold, was staggering
after the poignant scene that had just taken place. 'I
was carried away by—by a memory.'

Lexa said softly, looking up at him with shadowed
eyes,

'Your wife, Mr Mansell——'

'Don't mention her!'

'I feel it's better that I do,' she argued gently. 'She

died in a fire?' A question which she hoped he would
answer, so that he would believe it was him from whom
her knowledge came. And yet, all at once, it did not
really matter. It was told her in confidence, but as things
had turned out Lexa felt that to talk about his wife would
help him a great deal. So if he had not elected to answer
she would have told him what she knew. But he did
answer, telling her about the nanny who in her frenzy
had made no attempt to rescue the baby but had clawed
and dragged at him like a woman demented so that he
had no alternative than to go for his child first.

'The delay——' He shook from head to foot. 'It was
the delay that caused Sally's death. If only the nanny
had just acted with normal coolness and taken Alacho
from the nursery into the garden!' He paused, and Lexa
found herself hoping that he would not regret what he
was saying to her, would not feel any embarrassment or
loss of face. 'I was out, and had just come home when
I saw the fire, and Sally at an upstairs window, terrified
because she thought the bedroom door had jammed. It
did jam on occasions, but when at last I managed to get
up there it hadn't jammed—or if it had then it unjammed
again. The fire had come up through the floor and—and
Sally was—was——'

'Don't talk about it any more,' broke in Lexa gently.
'It's good that you've talked, but now——' She shook
her head in a firm little gesture. 'It's enough, Mr Mansell.' She glanced around. 'Let me get you a drink.
What would you like?'

He looked at her and she knew that he saw her this
time.

'I'll have a whisky—a double one.'

'It's in that cabinet?' She pointed, saw him nod and
went towards it. 'Here,' she was saying a moment later.

'Don't drink it too quickly, will you?'

He took the glass, and thanked her. She watched him gulp down the fiery liquid and frowned. She supposed there would be a temporary relief, but she did hope that he was not in the habit of taking whisky like this.

'You're a kind young woman, Miss Duke,' he said presently. 'First you saved Alacho, and then you comforted me.'

'I really did comfort you, then?' A lovely warmth came over her at the idea that she had been able to give him a little comfort. 'You really mean it?'

'I really mean it.' And to her amazement he smiled— for the first time she had known him. It was like a victory, she thought, smiling in response. 'Miss Duke, have a drink with me.' Imperious now his voice, with a return of the arrogance which was so very much a part of his general make-up. Lexa obeyed at once, going to the cabinet and pouring herself a small amount of brandy and filling the glass with dry ginger. She took it to the couch and sat down; Paul took possession of a chair facing her, his eyes on her face, then moving to her hair, and downwards with a swift sweep to glance fleetingly at her throat and shoulders and the tender curves of her firm young breasts. She coloured, recalling how she had been affected by him on the occasion when he had swum with her and Alacho in the sea, then chatted with her later, while his daughter played on the sands with another child.

It was over an hour later that Lexa said she must be going. She had not said the things she had come to say, but they could wait. She felt she had overstayed her welcome—if there was a welcome—and decided to leave Paul to his own thoughts, which was what he wanted.

'You won't brood?' she said impulsively, turning at the

door. 'Please promise you won't brood?'

A slight frown knit his brow.

'Does it matter all that much to you, Miss Duke?'

'Yes,' she nodded, 'it does.'

'Why?' His voice was rough, his eyes curious. 'My problems don't affect you, not in any way at all.'

She nodded mechanically, in agreement, moments of reflective silence going by before she spoke.

'You would resent anyone worrying about you?' Half question, half statement, and she looked into his eyes, hard dark eyes devoid of emotion, totally cold.

'It's not a case of resentment. I see no reason why you, a stranger to me, should take it upon yourself to show concern.'

The words hurt and she actually flinched.

'I'm not a stranger,' she argued. 'We've known each other for almost five months.'

'A superficial acquaintanceship.' Again his voice was rough, with that quiet burr absent. 'You'll have realised by now that I'm a man who doesn't mix, who doesn't need friends.'

Lexa's eyes flickered, a hint of censure in their soft violet-blue depths. She had turned back into the room, but the door was still open behind her and she was framed in it, a soft amber glow from the hall creating light and shade against her hair, her cheeks, the delicate curves of her body. It was a tense moment of wonder for them both, but it was only later—much later—that either of them realised it. The silence hung, suspended like a dream in the making, with only the quiet tick of a wall clock filtering through it, almost unnoticed. In Paul's throat that nerve pulsated; in Lexa's cheeks tender colour fluctuated for a brief moment, then faded, to leave her face pale—almost white.

The window was open slightly and suddenly there was a quivering movement of colour and life as a moth flew into the room, fluttering towards the light. The spell was broken and Lexa found her voice at last.

'It isn't that you don't need friends, Mr Mansell, it's just that you don't want them.'

He looked at her narrowly.

'You take liberties, Miss Duke,' he said curtly, eyes glinting with arrogance. 'My employees usually know their place.' He rose and stirred restlessly and, puzzled for a moment, Lexa wondered at the unexpected gesture, but perception came swiftly and she realised that he had suddenly accepted that his words just now scarcely fitted in with the intimate scene of a few moments ago when for slight comfort he had rested his head against the softness of her breast. She was beginning to know him, to penetrate the armour which protected his emotions. A curious sense of unreality accompanied this knowledge, because she had no definite objective in mind—she did not wish to probe, or to understand him. She wished simply to perform her role of nanny to his child.... Or did she?

Yes, consciously she did; it was all she wanted, life without complications, just as it had been for years—smooth, riding on an even keel. But subconsciously this man intrigued her; there was magnetism in his personality, power in his slim, muscular frame. He was handsome despite the scar; his self-confidence, his distinguished bearing, the impression he gave of superiority ... all these appealed to Lexa, had done from the first, even though her conscious mind had registered only dislike and, later, even hate, because of the way he treated his child, blaming her for the loss of his wife. It was unreasonable, the attitude of a man without any sense of rational judgement. Lexa had not been able to find any excuse for him, but now she was admitting that a man carrying the weight of grief which Paul Mansell carried was incapable of rational judgement. She frowned, and stared at him, silhouetted against the dim background beyond the window. She ought not to be making excuses for him! His wife was dead and nothing he could do or suffer would alter that. His child was alive, beautiful and ready to give him love in abundance.

And suddenly, out of the slight chaos of her thoughts, there came the sure conviction that she could bring the two together. Of the method she would adopt she knew nothing at present, but she did know that if endeavour could bring success then success would be hers.

The following morning she was up with the sunrise, looking from her bedroom window over the glory of the colour-garden to the wide lawns beyond and then to the beach of silver sand and the jetty where Paul's beautiful yacht was moored, its sails peach-pearl in the first glimmerings of a tropical dawn. The sea was smooth, like glass, the horizon dark but clear-cut against a sky about to ignite into a molten mass of colour. Lexa stood quite still, listening to the birds, her thoughts drifting back to last evening, to that intimate scene resulting from her impulsiveness, her overwhelming compassion for a soul in torture. She remembered Paul's coldness developing with every moment that she stayed, and she said again that she must go. He was embarrassed by what he would consider to be a loss of dignity, a lowering of his pride. To have allowed himself to derive comfort from a mere servant! How he hated it! Lexa had read it in his eyes.

Softly she had bidden him good night, turning to the door again, and had added in the same soft voice, repeating what she had said before, 'Please don't brood, Mr Mansell. It really isn't doing any good, you know.'

She saw him swallow, but whatever he felt inside was not revealed as his voice, curt and clipped, came across the room to her.

'Your concern is well-meant, Miss Duke, but I assure you it isn't necessary. As I said, you're kind. Please keep your kindness for my daughter; she needs it.'

Lexa hesitated, flushing at his words with their tangible sting which ought to have antagonised her. But, urged by some gentle perseverance too insistent to be ignored, she said engagingly,

'She needs love too—your love. In return she has so much to give, if only you'll accept it.' And without waiting for him to say anything she had left the room, closing the door noiselessly, then mounting the stairs to her bedroom.

Later, unable to sleep, she had gone to the window and for a few moments had gazed up at the star-spangled sky. Then a movement had attracted her attention, the hint of a shadow on the beach, visible beneath the palms. Pity encompassed her and she could have wept for his loneliness. He stopped suddenly and, turning, glanced towards the house ... almost as if he sensed being watched. Lexa drew back into the darkness of her room and got into bed, only to lie awake again, wondering if she could possibly succeed in the task she had set herself. If she did succeed, then Paul's loneliness would be gone for ever, and only memories would intrude now and then, memories that would fade eventually, blotted out by the love he would give to his daughter.

CHAPTER THREE

SHE did not see Paul again that week-end, for he had left even before she went down for an early breakfast. Maria, one of the maids, offered the information without a question being put to her.

'I'll have just rolls and jam, please, Maria.' Lexa felt unaccountably empty inside, knew a sense of loss because her employer had gone off like that, a whole day before he need have done. Reflectively she recalled —after that terrible scene involving Alacho—having wished he would curtail his visit, take himself off to Bangkok. But now that he had done just that she was feeling dejected, probably because she knew why he had gone, knew it was a direct result of what had occurred last evening. He had no desire to see her so soon after he had unbared his soul, accepted comfort, losing dignity in the process. And Lexa suspected he would not come over to Koh Kham next week-end, or even the one after that, and she proved to be right. He kept away, and although life ran smoothly without him there seemed to be something missing, a vital link both with the lovely house and the people in it. The servants' faces would drop when the phone call came through that their employer was not to be expected. Alacho, who had wanted to apologise, that first Sunday, when he had left so early, would go quiet on hearing that her father was not coming over. Yet with the resilience of youth she got over it, being happy enough, and there was a mischievous streak in her that was both exasperating and adorable.

Lexa loved her dearly, and desired only to have an
opportunity of proceeding with the task she had set herself. The opportunity, though, was never there, and when
Alacho, who despite her contentment and general enjoyment of her life with Lexa, the servants, and her dog,
Pango, asked if they could go to Bangkok to see her
father, Lexa gave the idea some consideration. That
Paul would not be pleased did quite naturally strike
her. But once they were there, in the hotel, he could
scarcely pack them off again immediately. He had never
forbidden Lexa to take Alacho to the city, so there
seemed no reason why she should not do so. True, lessons
would have to be neglected for a couple of days—as
they would have to stay the night—but the visit would
be educational anyway.

Alacho, believing that her suggestion had been ignored, indulged in those persuasive activities that invari-
ably got her what she wanted—at least with her nanny.
They were on the beach, drying off after having been in
the sea for a swim, and Alacho said, a smile on her
winsome little face,

'Are we going to see Daddy? I haven't had a holiday
from lessons for a long time—not like I did at school.
And I'm tired. I expect you are too, Auntie Lexa, so
why don't we go and stay at the hotel for a few days?'

'Suppose Daddy's very busy and can't be bothered
with us?'

'He might not be,' hopefully but with a lip quivering
all at once. 'Auntie Lexa, why doesn't he like me?'

'He does like you, silly——'

'He doesn't and you *know* it! Please let us go to see
him. I want him to like me.' A cry from the heart! Two
unhappy people, and all so unnecessary. Lexa knew a
flood of frustration at her own helplessness, and if she

had had any qualms about going to Bangkok they were dissolved by Alacho's next words. 'If he never hardly sees me how can he like me? I want to see him, Auntie Lexa. *Please* take me to him ... *please*!'

'Very well, pet, we'll go to see him.'

'Today?' Bright eyes and an eager voice. Alacho danced on the shore, clapping her hands together. Lexa smiled, looking up at her from the towel on which she was lying. The beautiful face with its petal-soft skin and peach-bloom colouring, the enormous brown eyes and wide forehead, the wealth of chestnut hair, curling naturally.... Lexa fell to wondering what her mother had been like.... 'Today, Auntie Lexa?' asked the child again, this time a trifle doubtfully.

'It's too late, darling, you know it is. We wouldn't get a boat.'

'Tomorrow, then?'

Lexa nodded.

'Yes, tomorrow.'

Should she telephone Paul? she wondered later, when she and Alacho were having tea in the nursery. No, she decided, since she was sure he would forbid them to come. Take him by surprise; as Alacho had so hopefully said, he might not be too busy to see them.

There was great excitement the following morning, with Alacho waking at the absurdly early hour of five o'clock.

'Go back to sleep,' ordered Lexa even while knowing she would not be obeyed. And so she got up twenty minutes later when she heard Alacho in the bath. Slipping on a dressing-gown she went to her.

'You wretch,' she said. 'There isn't a boat for hours yet!'

'There must be, because Daddy went off very early the last time he was here.'

'So he did; I'd forgotten. He went off before breakfast.'

'Shall we go off before breakfast, Auntie Lexa?'

'No, we won't. And, Alacho. . . .'

'Yes?' She glanced up from the depths of mountains of foam which came to her chin, and floated on her curls.

'You must stop calling me auntie. If Daddy doesn't like it then that's final, understand?' It was not often that Lexa adopted this kind of stern manner, but she felt it was very necessary.

'Then can I just call you Lexa? It's a beautiful name. Mine's beautiful, isn't it? You said it was pretty once. Can I call you Lexa?' she asked again, aware that she had diverted.

Lexa shook her head.

'No, Alacho, you can't, I'm afraid. Daddy wouldn't be at all pleased. In fact, I'm very sure he'd forbid it, and we don't want any more scenes, do we?'

Alacho lifted one leg and proceeded to sponge between her toes.

'No—he was going to beat me and that would have been cruel! You attacked him, and it was very brave of you.'

'I didn't attack him,' laughed Lexa, picking up a large bath-towel. 'I merely defended you. I don't expect he'd have spanked you, though——'

'He would!' interrupted Alacho forcefully. 'He was in a terrible temper. I don't know how you weren't frightened of him. I was!'

'Well, I must admit I wasn't at all happy with his anger. But it was all your fault, you know. It was only to be expected that he'd be angry with you, flying in to him like that and being so rude.'

'I did want to say I was sorry, though, the next morning, but he went away and I couldn't.' She was sponging the other foot, which she could hardly see for foam.

Lexa laughed and chided her about putting too much of the liquid in the bath.

'You waste it, Alacho. And it also makes it harder for Maria, who has to get rid of it before she can clean the bath.'

'The bath isn't dirty.'

'Come on out and less sauce! Have you washed your ears, and behind them?'

Alacho giggled.

'I always do!'

'You always don't! Let me have a look.'

Lexa got the flannel and did her ears.

'Ooh ... do you have to poke so much? You go deaf like that—a boy at school told me. You shouldn't wash your ears. Animals don't.'

'You're not an animal—— Step off the towel. How do you expect me to dry you?'

'I'm not having any lessons this morning, am I?' Alacho was pulling a dainty cotton dress over her head, standing before a pink-frilled dressing-table, looking at herself in the mirror as the dress was drawn down, over dainty panties of absurdly small dimensions.

'No; no lessons. Just breakfast and then the boat. You'll have to be patient, though, while I do the last-minute packing.'

'You did it all last night.'

'Not quite all.'

'Why did you put an evening dress in, Auntie Lexa——?' She stopped, putting a hand to her mouth. 'I can't call you Miss Duke now, I love you too much.'

Lexa smiled affectionately.

'Call me Lexa, then,' she said, aware that it was rash,

but uncaring anyway. Her job was safe; she was certain of it, so a few liberties, a few small acts of defiance could not jeopardise her position here. 'I really don't know why I put in an evening dress,' she said, answering Alacho's question. 'I don't expect I shall need it.'

'You might go to a dance after you've put me to bed.' Alacho picked up a hairbrush while Lexa fastened the buttons at the back of her dress. 'Shall I brush my own hair?'

'I'll do it.' Taking the brush from her, Lexa gave the lovely dark hair a vigorous going over before flicking the ends round Alacho's face.

'Do you think I'm pretty?' There was an impish light in the big brown eyes, a humorous curve to the little rosebud mouth.

'You're vain, that's for sure!' Lexa playfully tapped the top of Alacho's head with the hairbrush.

'Oh, you shouldn't do that! Not in Thailand!'

'Do what?' asked Lexa, puzzled.

'Tap anyone's head—or even pat it, like people do to children.'

Lexa blinked.

'Why not?'

'Because the Thai people say that the head's the highest part of the body——'

'Well, it is.'

'I know, silly! But they think the head's special and so if you pat it they'll not like you.'

'Is that right? You're not having me on?'

'No, I mean it's true.' She paused, concentrating. 'Oh, yes, I knew there was something else. When you go to a party or something like that you always try to put your head lower than other people's, so that they won't think you're being rude.'

Lexa looked at her sceptically.

'And how,' she enquired dryly, 'is everyone at a party going to get their heads lower than everyone else's?'

'Well....' Alacho frowned, then brightened. 'It's the young ones who have their heads lower, so that the older ones know you're respecting them! Yes, that's it—I remember now!'

'It sounds a charming custom. Do you know any more?'

'You have to take your shoes off when you go into a temple or into someone's nice house.'

'I knew that one. Come into my bedroom while I get on with the packing, and you can tell me of other customs, if you know any.'

Alacho stood by the bed watching the last few things go into the suitcase, and talked of other Thai customs, while Lexa listened with avid interest. She learned that Buddhist priests were forbidden to touch, or be touched by a woman. If she had any gift to make then she must first hand it to a man, or she could put it on to a handkerchief spread out in front of the monk. She learned that Thais don't shake hands, but they *wai* instead, which meant that they put hands together as if in prayer.

'I don't know any more——— Oh, yes! You never point your foot at anyone because the sole is the lowest part of your body, so it's an insult. Daddy told me to watch it if I crossed my legs in company because I might point my foot at someone.'

'And they'd be offended?'

'Yes, very much! But I can't always remember not to cross my legs.'

'Obviously you must try.' Lexa closed the lid of the suitcase and snapped the locks. 'There; we're ready. I only hope we can be fixed up for the night at the hotel.'

'Daddy has a few hotels, so we'll be able to stay at

one of them all right. Oh, I'm so excited! I love going to Bangkok!'

'You've been often?'

Alacho shook her head.

'Only four times. My other nannies wouldn't take me—they said Daddy wouldn't like it. One said he was a horrible man, so she left. Maria said it was because she fell in love with him, but I don't think anyone would leave because of that, do you?' Lexa was seeking in a drawer for handkerchiefs and a shoulder bag, so she said nothing. 'Would you fall in love with my daddy, Lexa?'

'Certainly not! What a question to ask, Alacho!'

'Sorry. But you don't think he's horrible, do you?'

'Stop asking silly questions. Have you got your bag?'

'I'll go and get it. It's the one to match my dress, isn't it?'

'Bring the white one, the shoulder bag.'

'All right.' Alacho went off happily, singing to herself. Lexa felt good. The sun was shining and the birds sang. Flowers bloomed everywhere on this island in the sun, this tiny bit of Thailand called Koh Kham, where the population was little more than a thousand people, most of them wealthy businessmen and their families, and most of them Thais, but there were a few foreign families too; among them, living along the beach from Paul's house, an English couple, retired. They had a daughter in England, married with four children, and an unmarried son, also in England. He was expected over for a holiday in a few weeks' time—this information came to Lexa from Mrs Bardsley whom she met on occasions either when on the beach or shopping in the little town, which in effect was just one main street with a little square in the middle of it.

Alacho came back with the bag over her shoulder.

'Will Pango be all right?' she asked anxiously.

'There are plenty of people here to look after him.'

'I'll bring him a lovely present back—a nice new collar!'

They arrived at the Ayudhya Palace Hotel in the afternoon after having taken the ferry and then a taxi. Although she was a little apprehensive about the coming meeting with her employer there was nothing in Lexa's manner to reveal it as she asked at the desk if he was anywhere about.

'He's at the Coral Tree in Rama IV Road,' she was told by the clerk. 'But he's staying here, so he'll be back for dinner.' He looked down at Alacho and smiled. 'You're quite a stranger,' he said.

'Yes, I haven't seen you for ages. Shall we go to the Coral Tree, Lexa? It's another of Daddy's hotels.'

'Perhaps we'd better wait until he comes back here.' Lexa turned to the clerk again. 'Can we have a room here? You're not full up?'

He seemed a little surprised by the question.

'Mr Mansell has a very large private suite, so I expect you'll be fixed up in that.'

'Oh, thank you. We'll be back later. My name's Duke—Miss Duke.'

'Very well, Miss Duke. I'll tell Mr Mansell you're here and that you'll be coming back later.' He beckoned to a porter and had the suitcase taken up to the suite. Lexa grimaced to herself, convinced that she would be hauled over the coals for all this. However, it was done now and the sensible thing was to begin enjoying it.

They stepped into the sunlit street and strolled south, coming to a fascinating Brahminic open-air shrine where Thais were offering incense and jasmine garlands. All the passers-by were *wai*ing—greeting each other with hands together as if in prayer, just as described by Alacho. Child-hungry women were offering wooden elephants ... and among it all were the camera-snapping tourists.

'Isn't it exciting!' Alacho's face was alive, her tiny feet dancing on the pavement. 'Can we go to see the Reclining Buddha? It's *enormous*, but I've never seen it. I asked Daddy to take me, but he wouldn't.'

Lexa, holding her hand, glanced down at her, quite unable to understand Paul Mansell's attitude towards his adorable child.

'Yes, we'll go and see the Reclining Buddha,' she returned gently, and hailed a cruising taxi which took them to Wat Po, the most extensive temple in Bangkok, and the one housing the vast Reclining Buddah, an image a hundred and sixty feet long and thirty feet high.

'I told you it was enormous,' said Alacho as they both stood, wide-eyed, looking at it. 'Why is he sleeping?'

'He's dying.' Lexa wondered how much gold leaf had been used in the covering of such a colossal figure. 'He's entering Nirvana, which means heaven.'

'Is Nirvana the Thai word for heaven?'

'It's the Buddhist idea of heaven.'

Alacho heaved a sigh.

'I wish I could come to Bangkok for a long holiday. There are so many other temples to see.'

'We shall come again,' promised Lexa as they came from the *Bot* into the courtyard where numerous saffron-robed Buddhist monks were moving about against an incredible backcloth of no fewer than three hundred and ninety-four gleaming sitting Buddhas.

'Can we stay a long time—when we come again, I mean?'

'We'll have to see what Daddy says, pet.' They were

wandering about the temple compound with its many bell-shaped *chedis* and sharp-towered *prangs* gleaming in the sunshine. 'I shall have to see if I can persuade him to let us stay for a week at least.'

'But not this time?' said Alacho wistfully.

'Well,' began Lexa doubtfully. 'I don't think so. You see, we've come without his expecting us, and he might not be pleased. You must be prepared for that, darling.' What a thing to have to say to a child!—having to warn her that her own father might not be at all pleased to see her.

The sun was lowering in the sapphire sky when they came away from Wat Po, and by the time they arrived back at the hotel it was blood-red, sinking into the 'River of Kings' between the travellers' palms of the hotel gardens and the vegetable sampans drifting slowly by on the river.

'Haven't we had a lovely afternoon?' Alacho's eyes were dancing as she spoke of the many things they had seen. 'Weren't the spirit houses beautiful? Every house and building has one,' she continued without giving Lexa time to reply. 'They're like little temples, aren't they? But they have to be because the "Lord of the Peace" spirit lives inside them—— Well,' she amended, 'it's his image carved on a piece of wood and they put it inside the house.'

'How did you come to know all this, Alacho?'

'Daddy told me, because one time when he brought me to Bangkok we saw them when we were in the car. They have to be on a pedestal—that's the long thing they stand on—and they have to be facing the light all the time because the spirit doesn't like the dark.'

'So Daddy does sometimes take you out with him?'

Alacho shook her head, the animation dying out of her face.

'It was only when he was taking me to the hotel.'

'I see. . . .' It had already occurred to Lexa that although Alacho had been to Bangkok four times previously, she had seen very little of it. She was later to learn that her father had merely brought her to the hotel and left her there in charge of one of the staff.

She and Alacho had alighted from the taxi and the driver had been paid off, but they stood for a space at the imposing entrance to the hotel, Alacho's hand clasped in that of her nanny, looking at the sun creating a play of colour, with the painted sampans moving languidly, as if their owners had all the time in the world. What a fascinating, mysterious and incredible city! A city of the senses—of sounds and smells, of the mystic charm of gold-gleaming temples and hundreds of meditating Buddhas, of happy smiling people.

Lexa said at last that they had better go in, but Alacho, with her customary intelligent interest in everything around her, wanted to stand a little longer. And when a street vendor offered her *chompoos* she took money from her shoulder bag and bought some, eating the skin and meat and dropping the small seeds into her hand. Lexa took them from her when she had finished eating the fruit and wrapped them in a tissue for getting rid of later.

At the desk again, Lexa was told that Mr Mansell had not yet returned, so she and Alacho sat in the lounge, each with a glass of iced lemonade on the table in front of her, brought by a waiter who seemed concerned that they were having to wait.

'It's all right,' Lexa assured him. 'Mr Mansell wasn't expecting us.'

The man smiled and went off. It was less than five minutes later that Lexa saw Paul, entering the lobby of the hotel accompanied by a tall, exquisitely-dressed woman of about thirty, a dark-haired beauty, poised, and with an air of arrogant assurance. Something seemed to turn inside Lexa, hurtful, affecting her pulse and nerves, then leaving her with a hollowness that was as uncomfortable as it was inexplicable. The two were walking close, but not speaking; they passed out of sight behind a cluster of potted palms and Lexa saw them no more.

She waited, angry that she had come, wishing she could go somewhere else, away from this opulent hotel, away from Paul, and that woman he was with.

Then she was experiencing puzzlement. He had no time for women; his whole life and thoughts were centred on the wife he had lost and on his business. Nothing and no one else had any interest for him, not even his daughter. So why was he with that woman———? Lexa pulled up her thoughts, aware of the absurdity of the conclusion she had so rapidly reached. The woman was merely an acquaintance, or perhaps a business associate. The wife of one of his hotel managers, maybe.

'I wish Daddy would come,' sighed Alacho ten minutes later. 'Can't you give him a ring at the Coral Tree and tell him we're here?'

'He'll be with us soon,' replied Lexa and at that very moment he appeared, alone, having been informed at the desk that his daughter and her nanny were waiting for him.

'What brought you here?' he demanded before she could speak. 'Is something wrong?' His grey eyes spared a casual glance for his daughter before returning to Lexa's face.

'We merely came on a visit,' she replied, trying to hold on to her calm. 'Alacho hasn't seen you for over a fortnight, so she asked me to bring her to you. I hope you don't mind? We shan't make a nuisance of ourselves, but we would like to stay here, if we may?'

Silence. He appeared to be staggered by her action. He sat down eventually and she saw that nerve fluttering, as she had seen it so often before. The scar was pale, strangely obscure. His eyes were on her, dark, inscrutable. They moved and she was conscious of their critical examination. She wore a classic, never-dating style of dress, small sleeves and shirt collar, tight bodice and skirt with flowing lines that brought out the richness of the print whose main colour was peacock blue subtly splashed with lime green and citrus yellow.

She lowered her lashes, unconsciously throwing shadows on to her face. The silence stretched and Lexa wished Alacho would find her tongue, if only to ease this tense and awkward moment. But it was Paul who spoke, saying quietly,

'Did it not occur to you to phone and ask my permission before bringing Alacho here?'

Lexa was honest enough to admit that this had occurred to her; she was also honest enough to add, lifting her eyes to his dark forbidding face,

'But I knew you'd probably put us off, and Alacho was very keen to see you. I do hope you have time to be with her, if only for this evening.'

He transferred his gaze to his daughter, sitting there, an empty lemonade glass in front of her. A smile fluttered to her lips, then faded beneath her father's masked expression.

'I'm a busy man.' Abrupt the tone, and the chiselled mouth was tight. 'How long had you planned to stay?'

Had. . . . Was he intending to send them home at once, then?—or rather, first thing in the morning, since it was too late now to make the journey.

'Only for a couple of days,' she answered. 'The desk

clerk said you have room. . . .' Her voice trailed to silence as he raised his brows.

'In my private suite?'

She swallowed hard, fast losing her confidence.

'Perhaps there's—there's a room in the hotel proper that—that we could have?' Her glance strayed to Alacho. Why was the child so tongue-tied? If only she would say something to her father! As if aware of Lexa's wish she did speak, saying that she had stayed in the suite last time and she would like to stay in it again.

'And there's plenty of room for Lexa, isn't there, Daddy?'

'Lexa?' he repeated, ignoring everything else.

'I said she could call me that, seeing that you didn't want her to call me auntie.'

'Lexa is even worse——' He stopped, and she had the odd impression that *his* use of her name angered him. Did he never want any name but Sally to pass his lips, then—at least, where women were concerned?

'She can't go on calling me Miss Duke,' said Lexa reasonably. 'And if *I* don't mind then why—why——' She stopped, colouring at the idea of what she had almost said. He finished it for her, saying slowly, deliberately,

'Then why should I? Miss Duke, you're impertinent!'

She looked away, recalling how he had lain his head against her breast in that moment of weakness, of desperation for comfort. It might never have been! The incident was forgotten as far as he was concerned. He was again her stern implacable employer whose word was law.

'I'm sorry if you think me impertinent, Mr Mansell. I don't mean to be. I feel that there are difficulties where my job is concerned, that you're finding me wanting in certain respects——' She stopped abruptly, frowning as she noticed Alacho's concentrated expression. 'Perhaps we could talk later, alone?'

He looked perceptively at her, then at his daughter. 'Very well,' he agreed, surprising her. 'Have dinner with me and we'll talk.' He seemed troubled, she thought, and it suddenly occurred to her that he was afraid she was thinking of giving up the post, hence the readiness with which he had agreed to talk. And they were dining together.... Lexa had brought a very charming dress, long, with an arresting mixture of flowers on a diagonally striped background. And in keeping with the flowing stripes and simple design of the dress she had chosen as her only jewellery a bracelet of gold with earrings to match. Her shoes were unpretentious black patent with high heels. She had had her hair set yesterday afternoon in preparation for this trip, and she felt elated— quite absurdly so, she told herself—by the idea that she would be looking her very best this evening when she dined in one of the hotel's splendid restaurants with her employer.

To her surprise he suggested they have tea; Alacho was delighted and it showed. Her father seemed interested in her reaction, in the light shining in her eyes, in the spontaneous way in which she danced along beside him when they all went from the lounge into the Tropicana Tea Bar. They sat in a corner, intimate, candlelit, for it was dark in the restaurant, with the sun falling so very swiftly outside. Palms and flowers and soft music.... A romantic atmosphere which seemed more suited to lovers. Alacho had been here before, though, and merely remarked on the new chairs and the curtains.

'I like them, Daddy. Did you choose them?'

'Of course not. I have people to do such things for me.'

'Oh ... you should pick things yourself. Next time I'll pick them if you like? We saw some lovely material today, didn't we, Lexa?' A swift glance at her father as the name came out. He was perusing the menu and seemed not to have noticed.

The tea was ordered—delicious sandwiches and French pastries. Lexa poured the tea from a silver-plated pot, while Alacho helped her father to sugar and then herself. Lexa did not take it.

It was a pleasant interlude, without strain and with Alacho chattering to her father in a way which Lexa had never witnessed before. She felt that if things could only go on like this the task she had taken on would prove to be much simpler than she had at first imagined.

When the meal was over they went into the gardens, which had a view to the river where lights flickered from the sampans and other boats, including some luxury yachts. Tall palms swayed against the darkening sky and away in the distance shadows blended to obscure the last lingering rays of pearl-grey light as the twilight made its swift descent. Soon lazy clouds drenched in moonlight would be sailing above the river and the brilliantly-lighted city.

There was a sort of gentle quietness about the grounds of the hotel which affected Lexa's senses so that she felt utterly at peace. The child chattering, the tall distinguished man beside her. . . . They seemed no longer part of it all, but beings aside, people she had just come across casually, as she strolled along. But the impression passed as swiftly as it had come and she was down on solid ground again, with all the little problems which her life presented. She asked about the room they would have, fully expecting to be put somewhere in the main part of the hotel.

'I ought to be getting Alacho to bed,' she explained.

'I'll take you up,' Paul said briefly, and they both followed him back into the hotel.

'It's Daddy's private lift,' Alacho said with a hint of pride. 'He doesn't use the others; they're for the guests.'

The suite was sumptuous, with a large, thickly-carpeted sitting-room, a super modern kitchen, three bedrooms and two bathrooms.

'There are two single beds in each of the spare rooms,' he said. 'You can share a room or have one each, whatever you prefer.'

'Perhaps we should share,' began Lexa, when she was interrupted by Alacho's saying she would like a room to herself.

'So you won't wake me when you come to bed,' she said with a swift affectionate smile. And so it was arranged, with Lexa finding herself in a room whose decor was in the most exquisite taste; the walls being silver-grey at the bottom shading gradually and subtly to white as they touched the ceiling. The carpet was Rosemary pink and the headboard of the bed, the stool by the dressing-table, and the low armchair all matched it. The bedspread was of a paler pink, embroidered in white.

Whose hand? wondered Lexa, automatically thinking of the woman with whom she had seen her employer. She shrugged. Stupid to speculate, to imagine things that would probably prove to be all wrong.

After washing Alacho's face and hands and seeing her into bed, Lexa began on her own toilet, taking a shower before putting on the dress and attending to her hair. She smiled faintly at her reflection when at length she was ready. Alacho had asked her to go into her room and this she did, watching the child's eyes widen to become bigger then ever, like saucers.

'You look lovely! Daddy'll like you—I think.'

'But you're not sure?' smiled Lexa, aware of a strange confusion of mind, an uneasiness which disturbed her even though its origin could not be grasped.

'He doesn't like any of my nannies, not usually.' A small pause as Alacho's eyes wandered over her figure. 'I think he'll like you, though. The others weren't beautiful and they didn't have lovely clothes like you.'

'Most of my clothes are just ordinary,' said Lexa, bending to draw up the cover which Alacho had rumpled and pushed down. 'Will you sleep? You don't seem at all tired.'

'I am, though. I shall think for a little while. I like thinking in bed; you can pretend you're in fairyland, and that you're a princes who's locked up in a castle in the sky and is rescued by a big tall prince——' Alacho stopped a moment and then, as if she had just made a discovery, 'Daddy's big and tall, and he'd be handsome like a prince if he hadn't got that horrid mark on his face. Do you think he had it when he was born? I knew a boy once who had a horrid red mark on his face and when I asked him what did it he said he had it when he was born. I'm glad I haven't——'

'I think, dear, that you've talked enough. It's late, and I mustn't keep your daddy waiting, must I?' The gentle tender tones brought an instant smile to Alacho's face and she sat up suddenly to plant a kiss on Lexa's cheek. 'Good night, darling; sleep well,' said Lexa tenderly.

'Good night, Lexa. I love you very much!'

CHAPTER FOUR

PAUL was waiting in the Orchid Lounge when Lexa came down. She saw him before he saw her and she stood for a moment in the shelter of a vine-draped trellis of bamboo and looked at him. He was leaning back in his chair, a glass in one hand while the other rested on the arm of the chair, his long slender fingers tapping unconsciously on the velvet upholstery. She saw his face in profile—set and severe, its lines taut, implacable. No movement; not a muscle, not even that familiar fluttering of the nerve in his neck. His face might have been a mask. The dark hair was brushed from his forehead, the threads of silver accentuated by the light from the tall candle on the table in front of him. She noticed his broad shoulders and the arrogant way his head was held above them, lending him an air of majestic superiority. He was dressed in off-white linen. The Ayudhya Palace was one of the few hotels in Bangkok where evening dress was required.

Lexa moved at last, and it did seem that he sensed her approach, for he turned his head long before she reached him, and she saw the expression in his eyes, the fleeting interest, the same fleeting look of admiration, the swift sliding glance that took in everything about her in one comprehensive sweep. He had risen from his chair immediately on seeing her, and was waiting for her to sit down.

'I'm sorry I'm late, Mr Mansell,' she said, 'but I stayed with Alacho a little longer than I intended.'

'That's all right; we have the whole evening. What will you drink?'

'A dry sherry, please.' She ventured a glance from under her lashes as he turned to beckon a waiter. So attractively distinguished! Almost magnificent, with those noble, clear-cut features and dark grey eyes, the firmly-chiselled mouth above a jutting chin, and that quiet, natural air of assurance. Lexa noticed several women glancing at him, repeatedly, as if they found it impossible to keep their eyes off him. The sherry was brought and placed on the table in front of her; she picked up the glass, sipped the amber liquid, then put it down again. Paul handed her a menu and began to peruse one himself. Lexa knew they were dining in the Normandie Grill which was on the twenty-second floor, with a magnificent view of the river from its roof-top location. She felt excited, expectant. This was the kind of living she had read about but never thought to experience; it was luxury at its greatest and she was thrilled to be here, in this fantastic hotel, with the most handsome man she had ever met. Yes, she had come to realise just how good-looking he was in spite of the scar. In fact, it seemed now to be so much a part of him—an essential part—that she scarcely regarded it as a blemish at all. The scar on his hand was negligible; she noticed it as he held the menu, and thought with a little inward shudder just how much worse his injuries could have been. How brave to enter a burning house! But the action would never have surprised her; it was what she would have expected from a man like Paul Mansell, whose very personality spoke of courage.

'Have you decided?' His voice filtered through her wandering thoughts and she brought her attention back to the menu.

'I'm so confused by such things as Shin Sun Lo Soup and Bang Poo Crab and Smoked Pla Krapong. Then there's Kuchurnpuan. Is that the way you pronounce it?' Her eyes were alight with laughter and although he also seemed amused he did not smile. But when he spoke his voice was no longer abrupt.

'That's correct. And there's no mystery about Kuchurnpuan. In plain French it's merely *hors d'oeuvres*. However, you won't be eating any of those. Tonight in the Grill we're offering a classical French cuisine prepared by our Swiss chef.'

'Oh, I have the wrong menu, then?'

He nodded, holding out his hand for it. He passed her his own, saying that he had not noticed it when he gave it to her.

'The waiter ought not to have brought it in the first place,' he ended before calling to the waiter who happened to be passing.

'I'm sorry, Mr Mansell,' he said when the mistake had been pointed out to him. 'It must have got in with the others.'

Lexa and her escort were conducted to a table positioned similarly to the one they had occupied on that first day, but this restaurant was even more luxurious than the Mandarin Grill, being designed for dining at night, in a romantic setting with candles and flowers everywhere. There were glorious colours—flaming lilacs and sage-brown blossoms tumbling over the walls of a miniature decorative blockhouse at one corner of the room; an orchid wilderness forming a foil for a water-garden complete with fountain and statuary—all in Thai fashion. Potted palms and other foliage plants, bamboo-work, hidden lights in subtle, mystic colours. Gold-skinned waiters in gleaming white coats, crystal glass and the beautiful copper-bronze cutlery famous to Thailand. Lexa, lost in a dream world of unreality, wondered vaguely what she would feel like were she to be here, in this highly romantic setting, with a man she loved. She looked at her companion, at his fixed, austere expression, and a tiny sigh escaped her. She would never be lucky enough to find herself in a place like this with a man she loved, simply because, if she ever did fall in love, it would be with someone who could never afford this kind of luxury. In any case, there was no chance of her falling in love while she was in Thailand; she had a job of work to do which would take up all her time for several years to come.

There was a small branch of candles on the table, and beside her plate an orchid in a tiny container. Close by was a pin. She glanced at the orchid but was too shy to pick it up and pin it to her dress. Paul brought her attention to the omission, but she said, fingering the exquisite bloom with what could only be described as a caress,

'I think it's a shame to take it from the water.'

The steely grey eyes became perceptive.

'You surprise me by your shyness, Miss Duke. I notice that you're never shy when talking to me,' he added with dry sarcasm which went right home, bringing the colour to her face.

'There's no parallel,' she retorted, and he immediately said,

'You see what I mean?'

She had to laugh, albeit a little shakily.

'I was a schoolteacher for four years,' she said at length, 'and I found I just had to hold my own with complaining mothers.'

Paul leant back in his chair, eyeing the wine waiter

for an instant as he put a bottle of dry white wine in the ice-bucket by the table.

'Do they often complain?' he asked, surprising her. She wondered if he were talking for talking's sake, but his expression was now one of interest.

'Not often. There's usually a pleasant, friendly rapport between teacher and parent; there has to be, as the child is between the two and it would suffer if they were at loggerheads.'

'But they do complain sometimes?'

She nodded, quite oblivious of the fact that the candle-light, catching her hair, turned it to spun gold, or that the man opposite to her was angry with himself for noticing ... and admiring.

'Yes, they do, usually for the most trivial thing.' She went on to tell him what some of the complaints were, then stopped to say accusingly,

'Mr Mansell, you can't really be interested. Why have you made me talk like this?'

'I know so little about you,' he said. 'I'd like to know more, so carry on talking, please.'

She shook her head, frowning.

'Why do you want to know more about me?'

'It's very simple. You're my child's nanny.'

'You engaged me without knowing much about me,' she reminded him, and he nodded in agreement.

'I took a chance,' he told her. 'I'd interviewed many women and I was becoming bored with the repetition. They were all the same, interested mainly in the fact that the job offered travel to the Orient and a long stay there. It was something different, adventure. Some asked about holidays, salary, whether a car would be provided and if so when would they use it? How much time would they have off during the week? Very few thought to ask about the actual job and what it entailed. Not one seemed interested in the child herself.' A glint had come to his eyes. Lexa read contempt there and could fully understand his feelings.

She maintained a silence even after he had finished speaking and several minutes passed before he said, his voice quiet, attractive, his face softened by the candle-light,

'Go on talking, Miss Duke. Tell me about yourself. I know a little both from the interview I had with you and from Miss Saunders, but I know nothing of your background.'

Was he genuinely interested, and if so, why? His explanation was of course feasible: he wanted to know more about her because she was his child's nanny. Yes, a feasible explanation but not an acceptable one, not the way he was with Alacho, caring nothing for her, indifferent to the love she offered. She heard him say again, 'Tell me about yourself, Miss Duke.'

She fingered the exquisite little container holding the orchid, then tenderly touched the flower itself, marvelling at the beauties of nature.

'It's difficult to talk about oneself,' she said, and for the second time since she had known him she saw him smile. But it was nothing more than a sardonic curve of his lips, she realised after a moment, and waited for some stinging comment. However, he merely said,

'You're the first woman I've known who doesn't like talking about herself, Miss Duke.'

Her eyes met his; she wondered if he was aware that her thoughts had flown to his wife. Had *she* liked talking about herself? If so, her husband had obviously loved to listen. Some strange yearning came to Lexa as she continued to look at him, and to think about his wife. Some

island is being developed and I'm building an hotel there.'
His eyes hardened, as if a memory angered him.

'It's a beautiful part of the world.'

'I like it.'

'You'd never live in England again?'

He stiffened and she saw one hand clench over the handle of his fork. The scar became livid.

'No,' he replied harshly, 'I shall never live in England again.'

His dead wife. . . . He had been happy in England with her and now that she was gone he couldn't bear to live there any more. But he had returned for that holiday and to get a nanny for his child. A temporary visit, and Lexa knew instinctively that it would be a long time before he visited the country again.

The second course duly arrived and after that the tension seemed to ease within Lexa while Paul, too, became more relaxed as they sat eating excellent food and listening to old-style Thai music played by accomplished musicians on ancient traditional instruments. Then came a display of classical Thai dancing, the girls' movements graceful, exquisite, with every gesture meaning something. Their costumes glittered and Paul told Lexa that the headdresses could take half an hour or more to arrange.

When the dancing finished couples could get up. Lexa, an excellent dancer, looked at the one or two who had taken the floor, then at her companion. His face was dark and set, his expression inscrutable, but Lexa knew instinctively that his thoughts were even yet again with the woman he had loved—and still loved.

'Let's go now.' He looked across at her enquiringly. 'There's nothing else you would like—more coffee?'

'No, thank you.'

He had not even mentioned Alacho, or the visit, and Lexa just had to say,

'You're not vexed that we came, are you?'

'I don't think it really matters,' he answered, surprising her. 'It will be a change for you both.' And that was all. They went from the restaurant to the lift, which took them down to the Garden Bar, a cosy outdoor bar set in the tropical garden with its extensive lawn overlooking the river, the lazy river where lights twinkled from the fishing boats ... so many of them. Wonderful seafood came from the Gulf of Siam.

'Will you have something to drink?' Paul beckoned a waiter as he asked the question. Lexa would have preferred not to drink any more but felt he would be more comfortable if she did, for obviously *he* intended having a drink. She told him her preference and it was ordered. He said, when it had arrived and all was quiet around them,

'Miss Duke, you're not thinking of leaving, are you?'

So it had been on his mind all the time! She shook her head instantly, and smiled at him reassuringly.

'I'm quite settled and happy in my job, Mr Mansell.'

'Thank you,' softly, and with an unmistakable hint of gratitude coming through to her. 'I had a feeling that you were discontented about something.'

'Because I said there were difficulties regarding my job?' He merely nodded and she went on, eager now that the subject she wanted to talk about had been broached, 'I said you found me wanting in some respects——'

'*I* haven't said so.'

'You've implied it, though.'

'I dislike familiarity. Alacho ought not to be calling you Lexa.'

'What difference does it make? She's happier because, as she says, it's more friendly.'

'And you——?' The dark eyes met hers, reluctantly, she thought, as if to look at her was to see things he would rather not have noticed about her. 'Don't you demand total respect? I thought all schoolteachers did.'

'Alacho does give me respect, all I want from her. Friendship is just as important. Surely you will agree with me there.'

'What are you trying to say, Miss Duke?'

She did not hesitate.

'Don't you ever want friendship from your daughter, Mr Mansell?' Persuasive her voice, and rather gentle. He moved as if uneasy, and a slight frown creased his brow. Had she set him thinking? She hoped so, for that would at least be a start. 'She's a lovely child,' she added perseveringly when he did not speak. 'You're all she has . . . and she's all you have. . . .' Her voice trailed softly down to silence and she saw his eyes raised from their contemplation of the glass he held.

'It isn't possible for me to love her,' he said at last, shaking his head. There was a hopeless, brooding quality in his tone as he added, 'If it wasn't for her, if she'd never been born, then my wife would be with me now.'

'I can't agree,' was Lexa's intrepid rejoinder. 'As a fatalist, I believe that we all go when our time comes. It was fated that your wife was to die at that time——'

'No, no, you're wrong,' he broke in forcefully. 'Nothing can alter the fact that, had I been only a minute sooner, I could have saved my wife.'

Lexa gave an exasperated sigh.

'As I've said, I don't agree. However, even if you *are* right and I am wrong, is it Alacho's fault that her mother died? She never asked to be brought into the world——'

She stopped, hesitating, watching his expression to see if she dare continue. But she had gone so far and she added quietly, 'You were responsible for her coming into the world—you, Mr Mansell.'

He glowered at her, his mouth tight.

'You're very brave, Miss Duke,' he said icily. 'Don't go too far. Your confidence that I depend on you appears to have given you the idea that you can say what you like and that I shan't dismiss you.' He looked directly at her, his eyes points of steel. 'No one is indispensable; keep that in mind.'

'I'm sorry,' she murmured, thinking of the child, and the blow she would receive were her father to deprive her of the love which she was receiving from her nanny.

He seemed ready to forget the matter on receiving Lexa's apology, and the rest of the evening was spent in amicable conversation. She listened avidly when he told her about the attractions of other parts of Thailand.

'You can visit ancient capitals, now in ruins,' he said. 'And there are lovely beach resorts and desert islands. We have beautiful jungle scenery, spectacular limestone caves at Kanchanaburi. There's Chiang Mai five hundred miles to the north of here—you'd have to take time off to do a trip like that, of course, but we might arrange it some time. There, you can visit the hill tribes who live in primitive jungled mountain villages.' He went on to describe other places, such as the jungles of the River Kwai, where one could see the world-famous bridge, and visit the war cemetery of the Allied soldiers who built the 'Death Railway'. Lexa thought about the nine thousand British, American, Australian and Dutch soldiers who had died during the building of that railway and shook her head, frowning as she looked at Paul.

'I'd never want to see the bridge, or the cemetery,' she

said huskily. 'In fact, I don't think the cemetery should be treated as a tourist attraction.'

'Nor do I,' he agreed, but went on to say that perhaps it did do some good, if only because it brought home to people the horrors, and the futility, of wars. But she was shaking her head.

'Men have waged wars since they came on the earth, and they'll go on waging wars——' She spread her hands in a kind of exasperated gesture. 'Why is it that they have this obsession to kill?'

His expression had undergone a change while she spoke and his gaze was now curious, interested, and lacking the hard metallic look which she had seen so often, and which seemed to be so much a part of him.

'You hate violence,' he murmured. 'So do I, but how is one to put a stop to it?'

'The only way would be to change man's character, and that's impossible.'

'By man's character, do you mean the human race as a whole?'

'Oh, no,' she returned swiftly. 'I mean only the male of the species.'

To her surprise she noticed a shade of amusement touch the chiselled outline of his mouth.

'Men are violent, then, but never women?'

'A few women have been known to be violent,' she admitted, 'but their numbers are infinitesimal compared to the men who have been violent.' She paused, then said, 'I don't like this subject, Mr Mansell, and I don't think you do, either.'

'No,' he agreed, 'there are other, more pleasant subjects.'

She looked at him and smiled. He seemed to want her company and the idea thrilled her in a way she could not understand. On the whole it had been a most pleasant evening, and although her employer's attitude could hardly be described as friendly, it was certainly more affable than ever before. Also, he had not minded her coming here, bringing his daughter to see him. Would he spend some time with her? wondered Lexa, refusing to lose hope in spite of his disheartening reaction when she broached the subject of his child. He had stated firmly that it wasn't possible for him to love her, but Lexa in her optimism was by no means convinced. He had never been brought close to the child; no one had ever been interested enough to want to help either him or Alacho and so, from the very first, there had been a wide gulf between them, with Paul living his introversive life and Alacho in the care of a nanny. The gulf had widened, as inevitably it would have done under circumstances like those, but now ... now, Lexa meant to narrow that gulf, and eventually to close it if she could.

However, during the visit she made no headway at all, and a few days later she was feeling very low in spirit as she put one of Alacho's dainty handkerchiefs on the board and began to iron it. She and the child had been allowed to spend four days in the capital, and had been provided with transport for the whole of the time, but not once had Paul accompanied them on their sightseeing trips, which had been to more temples, to the Floating Market—an incredible array of boats laden with every conceivable kind of fruit and vegetable and other commodities. They had sailed down to the ancient capital of Thailand and seen the magnificent ruins, and finally they had visited the famous Rose Garden where, in fifty acres of tropical luxuriance, they had witnessed some of the sports and traditions of the country, Alacho being delighted with the elephants at work pushing massive logs into the river, the folk dancing, the sword-fighting; and especially she had been thrilled to see a typical Thai wedding ceremony in which she had actually been invited to take part. All this ... and not once had Paul succumbed to the persuasions offered both by his daughter and by Lexa herself.

'I have work to do,' he had snapped, and on that occasion Lexa had accepted his refusal as final. Useless to bother him further. But he was not working all the time. One evening when Lexa had let Alacho stay up and dine with her they had been in a secluded corner of the restaurant when Paul entered, with the woman Lexa had seen him with before. She heard the woman's voice as they passed, Paul unaware she was there, with his daughter who at that moment was chatting with the waiter, a young man whom she knew from previous visits to the hotel. The voice, English, was husky and low, and as Lexa watched, the woman placed a hand on Paul's sleeve, possessively, and turned a perfectly made up, smiling face to his, appearing not to be in the least put out by his fixed, unsmiling countenance. A stab of dejection struck Lexa and stayed there. She felt it would be politic to move before Alacho saw her father, or he saw them. Alacho had been surprised, reluctant to go somewhere else and naturally wanting to know why. However, she agreed in the end and they left the restaurant and went to one of the others in the hotel.

'We shall be too long here,' she had said by way of excuse for her action. 'Dinner takes time and I can't keep you up too late.'

So Paul had no idea that Lexa had seen him with the woman, a woman who *might* be a business acquaintance, but Lexa rather thought she was something more than that. Yet this conclusion did not fit at all with the fact that he still pined after his dead wife. Alacho had said quite definitely that he did not like ladies very much. However, Alacho could not know what went on when he was away from home, which was for most of his time. Lexa thought of his comparative youth, of a body that was clearly healthy and virile, and she was forced to own that a man like Paul would have the natural desires of sex, and that being so he would surely take a woman for his mistress. Marriage, mused Lexa, was out, so if the woman had any ambitions in that direction she was doomed to disappointment.

Lexa took up another handkerchief, a sigh on her lips. She was speculating, imagining, putting her own personal conception on to the situation and she was, in all probability, quite wrong. This she had decided on the first occasion when she had seen her employer with the woman. She would forget the matter altogether, she determinedly told herself—and a moment later was thinking of Paul and that woman and wondering just what they were to one another.

Alacho came dancing in just as Lexa finished her ironing, her face wreathed in smiles.

'I'm invited to a tea-party! Guess where?'

'I can't guess. Who have you been talking to? I told you to stay in the garden and play with Pango.'

'I know, and I promised, but Pango ran off, along the beach right up to the Bardsleys' house, and I had to go after him. Mrs Bardsley's got four grandchildren staying at her house and Stella's having a birthday on Tuesday, so I'm invited. Can I have a new dress, please, with frills on it, and I want some white socks as well.'

'I didn't know the Bardsleys had visitors. I saw Mrs Bardsley just before we went away and she didn't say anything.'

'They came yesterday! They came with their uncle—I don't know his name but he's Mrs Bardsley's son—and Mr Bardsley's as well,' added Alacho as an afterthought.

Lexa looked at her, looked into the beautiful brown eyes, into the delicate little face with its adorable rose-bud mouth ... and yet again she wondered what her mother was like.

'Have you seen this gentleman, the uncle?'

'Yes, he was walking with Mrs Bardsley on the beach. He's nice, with lovely wavy hair and nice white shorts and a T-shirt like that one of mine with blue stripes.' Alacho picked up the little pile of handkerchiefs from the end of the ironing-board. 'Shall I take these and put them in a drawer?'

'If you like. This party's on Tuesday, you say?' It was almost a full week away, thought Lexa, and wondered how Alacho would contain her impatience.

'Yes, and we're having jelly and cakes and lemonade!'

'And how do you know that?' asked Lexa, laughing.

'I asked Mrs Bardsley and she said it wouldn't be a proper party without jelly—I *am* having a new frock, aren't I?'

'Of course. We'll go into town tomorrow and see what we can find. Didn't you see any of Mrs Bardsley's grandchildren?'

'No, they'd gone somewhere with their mummy and daddy—on a picnic, I think. I might see them tomorrow.'

'I thought you said they'd come with their uncle.'

'They did, but with their mummy and daddy as well.' Alacho went off with the handkerchiefs and the next Lexa saw of her was when she glanced from the nursery window. She was with one of the gardeners, the dog lying at her feet. She would be all right for a while, decided

Lexa, who wanted to do a little ironing of her own. It was while she was engaged on this that Maria came to her and said,

'Mr Mansell's just phoned to say he wants a few clothes sending on to the hotel, but I can't find some of them.' She looked worried as she brought forth the list which she had made out according to his instructions over the telephone. 'Will *you* look, Miss Duke, just so I can be absolutely sure they're not there?'

'You mean—go into Mr Mansell's bedroom?' Lexa shook her head as she spoke. 'I wouldn't like to do that, Maria.'

'It won't matter,' said the maid, a little puzzled by Lexa's reluctance. 'I just want to be sure I haven't missed them. There's a white evening shirt and a blue one. Neither of those are anywhere that I can see.'

'You want me to come now?' Lexa automatically turned the heat controller on the iron to cool. She was still reluctant to go into her employer's room, but as Maria had said, it didn't really matter.

'There's no desperate hurry. The parcel can't go on a boat today as there isn't one.'

'I'll take a look later, then. Two shirts, you say, one white and one blue?'

'Yes, and a pair of light grey linen slacks—— Here's the list. I've ticked off what I found, so all the others are missing. I think he must have them with him already.'

'That's possible,' agreed Lexa, glancing at the list. 'However, I'll have a search for them when I have time.'

'I'll be sending off the parcel tomorrow afternoon.'

'All right. I shall look before then—tomorrow morning, probably.'

It was later that day that she met Mrs Bardsley's son, Jeremy, a tall good-looking young man with frank blue eyes and thick fair hair. Lexa guessed his age to be about twenty-six or seven. He was an architect, he told her. They met on the beach when Lexa was walking along it with Alacho and the dog. He and his parents were sun-bathing after having been in the sea.

'Mother told me about you,' he said when they had been introduced. 'How are you liking Thailand?'

'I love it.' She liked him on sight and suspected he liked her too. They met again that evening after she had put Alacho to bed. She often took a stroll along the beach, so this was no exception. The tall figure appeared out of the shadows into the moonlight and she recognised Jeremy instantly.

The pleasure on his face when they came up to one another was flattering, to say the least, and Lexa found herself anticipating a walk that was much more enjoyable than those she had been taking on her own. She and Jeremy seemed to have a lot in common and they talked and talked for what seemed hours before she exclaimed, looking at her watch by the light of the moon,

'Good heavens! It's past eleven o'clock. We must have walked back and forth along the beach dozens of times! I must be going.'

'Need you? It's been great talking to you. I've got my sister and brother-in-law, and Mum and Dad, but no nice girl to call my own, as it were.'

She laughed.

'You mustn't call me your own,' she returned lightly. And then, 'When will you be leaving?'

He grimaced.

'That's not very tactful of you, child! I've only just come.'

'Oh, dear....' She laughed again. 'I didn't think, and yet I ought to have because I'm so used to mothers saying, if they met me in town only the day after we broke up for school holidays, "Hello, Miss Duke. Enjoying your break? What date does school open again?"'

Jeremy laughed heartily.

'Loving parents ... but they'd rather have their kids off their hands. Poor you! Aren't you glad you gave it up in favour of being a nanny on this beautiful island?'

'I'm enjoying it, but I also enjoyed teaching. Infants are adorable—eager to learn and not yet old enough to be assertive or cheeky to their elders. I shall be going back to teaching one day, obviously.'

'You will? Why?' They were strolling back towards that part of the beach which was Paul's private property, strolling in the moonlight where palms waved against the sky and the sand was like silk beneath their feet.

'Well, Alacho won't need me for ever, will she?'

'For years, though.'

'After that I must leave here, and take up teaching again.'

'Nonsense! You'll be married—probably long before Alacho's stopped needing you.' He was very close; he ventured to put a hand beneath her elbow and she glanced up into his face. 'Surely you want to be married with a family of your own?'

'I suppose every woman wants that,' she admitted, but went on to say that the right man hadn't yet turned up, and it was getting a little late.

'Late?' He laughed at that and said, 'You're no more than twenty-two—— Oh, you must be. You told me you were teaching for four years. Well, whatever your age you don't look it. And as for the right man not having turned up yet ... well, you never know.'

'Don't be silly,' she said, because she was embarrassed by the implication.

'We've only just met—yes, say it, and then tell me what difference it makes.'

'You have to get to know people.'

'We've time. I'm here for a month.'

'A whole month!'

'I take a holiday once a year and have it all together. Can't abide short breaks like some people have. I'd rather wait and look forward to the month.'

'Will you stay here all the time, on Koh Kham, I mean?'

'I'll go off to Bangkok once or twice. Coming with me?'

'Don't be silly,' she said again. 'I'm a working woman!'

'You have a holiday, surely?'

'Perhaps; later. I've only been here a few months, though, so I shan't be getting holidays for some considerable time.'

'Bring the kid with you.'

'Alacho's father would never agree to that.'

'He's an odd bod, so Mum tells me. Morose, an introvert—would be a hermit, she thinks, if it weren't for his interest in his business. She tells me he hasn't much time for the child. That right?'

Lexa frowned.

'Please don't talk like that about my employer, Jeremy. He has his own way of living and it's nothing to do with anyone else.'

'Snub goes home! Sorry; remind me if I get on the subject again.' They had reached the gate leading to the grounds of Paul's house and Lexa stopped. The moon was high, rolling along against the clouds, its argent glow painting the lawns and fountain and the wide borders of exotic flowers. Lexa inhaled deeply the perfume of the scented star jasmine and saw in her mind's eye the dainty tufted white flowers whose scent, it was said, from one plant alone, could spread perfume over an acre of ground. The lines of the gracious house were sharply etched against the starlit sky, its shadowed arches stimulating the imagination. The entrance was floodlit, its white marble columns gleaming like mother-of-pearl.

'He's got a fabulous place here,' commented Jeremy. 'But then he can afford it. I wonder what happened to his wife. He's never mentioned her to anyone as far as Mum knows. Divorced?'

'No——'

'Widowed, then?'

'Yes,' abruptly as Lexa reached for the gate latch. 'I must be off——'

'Why? The boss isn't at home, you were saying.'

'You said to remind you if you spoke of my employer again.'

'I only meant—— Oh, never mind. If you must go you must. Can I see you tomorrow some time?'

'Well....'

'Sorry if I said things I shouldn't, Lexa. Forgive and forget. I didn't mean to be churlish in any way at all. Say you'll see me.'

She turned to him, pushing open the gate at the same time.

'Alacho has her lessons in the morning, but we don't work in the afternoons. We shall probably be on the beach at around four——'

'Four o'clock? That's late.'

'I know, but I've promised to take Alacho into town for a party dress.'

'Oh, the party. A crazy idea, because there aren't enough children round here for a party.'

'There are about eight that I can think of,' she said. 'Four o'clock, then, on the beach?'

'If it has to be,' resignedly, and with a little shrug. 'And in the evening . . . can we walk like this again?'

She hesitated a moment, plainly detecting the thread of pleading in his voice but as yet unsure of her own desires. He was going too fast for her, she thought, trying to sink her doubts and remember the pleasure she had already had from his company. At last she agreed to walk with him but added, trying to inject a note of severity into her voice,

'Don't jump to any conclusions, Jeremy. This is merely a friendly relationship.'

'Okay, as you will. Tomorrow at four—somewhere under the palms along there.'

She left him, her mind confused. She liked him, but wished he had been a little more reserved. Perhaps she was old-fashioned; both men and girls seemed to work faster these days—where human relationships were concerned, that was.

As she mounted the stairs her thoughts switched to Paul, and then by a natural progression to the clothes he wanted sending to the hotel. She was not in the least tired and after glancing in to see that Alacho was sleeping peacefully she went quietly along to Paul's bedroom. The servants were all quiet, some of them already in bed and others in the kitchen, talking together as they usually did. There were three maids and two gardeners, all of whom lived in. The chauffeur and his family lived in a small house in the grounds, well away from the house.

She pushed open the bedroom door, surprised to feel her heartbeats increasing, as if she were engaging herself in some disreputable act. The room was flooded with moonlight, but she switched on the main light and, moving to the window, pulled the silken cord that drew the curtains across it, shutting out the moon and the panoramic view of the sea and the other tiny islands floating on it.

Where to look first? The drawers, of course. No result. The wardrobes—there were three huge ones all along one wall. She found a white shirt hanging up, hidden from view because it had got squeezed between several other shirts. Yes, that looked like one. And now for the other, and the slacks. The latter were definitely not here, but she did find the other shirt. She stood then, concentrating on that list, which she had omitted to bring with her. There was something else.... Ah, yes, a green linen jacket. Well, that certainly wasn't here—— Another chest of drawers by the bed caught her eye and even though she was sure the coat could not possibly be in any of those she nevertheless decided to take a look, opening the bottom drawer first, and then the middle one. It would not be in the top one, she thought, pulling it out all the same.

A photograph lay on top of a book, the photograph of a beautiful girl.... Lexa closed the drawer swiftly and, picking up the garments, she left the room, switching off the light as she did so.

His wife.... She knew it without any doubt at all. But why did he have it there—where any of the maids could see it. Suddenly Lexa found her brain registering the fact that the drawer in question was the only one with a lock. The key was not in the lock.... Had Paul believed he had locked the drawer, before he went away? The following morning when she delivered the clothes to Maria she said,

'Does Mr Mansell keep anything under lock and key?'

'He keeps the top drawer of his bedside cabinet locked, always, but I think there's only his private papers in there. The slacks and coat wouldn't be in there anyway.'

Always locked.... He'd taken the key; he believed the drawer was locked....

All morning Lexa was preoccupied, scarcely able to attend to Alacho even when she asked questions.

That drawer seemed to fascinate her. Last night her conscience had forbidden even a second glance at the picture, but now ... now she was curious, almost desperately so.... To take a look could not do any harm....

CHAPTER FIVE

THE curtains were still drawn, so none of the maids had been into the room for the past two days. Yes, for two days Lexa had fought her desire to look at the photograph, but now she had succumbed, again telling herself that it could do no harm. Alacho had been in bed for a mere half hour, and Lexa was to meet Jeremy at half-past eight. She had had her meal with the child, as usual, at half-past five, and had read to her since then, both before putting her to bed and afterwards. She was almost asleep when Lexa left her a few minutes ago, intending to take a shower and change in readiness for her meeting with Jeremy. They were to visit a little café at the end of the beach and just a little way inland, where they would have a drink and perhaps a snack. They had been there last evening, after strolling on the sands for over an hour. Jeremy had talked about his job, his bachelor flat, his friends and business acquaintances. He'd had several girl-friends, but there had never been anything serious. Lexa told him about her parents, her job at the school, her life as part of the village community. Many exchanges between them, and one swift kiss ... as they parted at the gate last night....

Lexa switched on the light, aware that her every movement was furtive, result of a guilt complex. This was wrong ... but who would know? It wasn't prying, because she could have looked the other night—she *should* have done so, because then the desire would have been satisfied and she would not be here now.

81

She could never have explained the overwhelming force of curiosity that propelled her; she only knew that right from the first she had wanted to know what Alacho's mother was like.

She pulled open the drawer and lifted the photograph, holding it with both hands as if it were some precious piece of porcelain. How beautiful! The flawless bone structure and skin, the contours of throat and shoulders. . . . The hair was a glory of auburn-brown—like beech leaves in autumn; the eyes, clear and honest, were large, the same colour as Alacho's. Lexa estimated the girl's age at about nineteen or twenty when this photograph was taken. Was she married then, or had she given this to Paul while they were going out together—engaged, perhaps? She turned it over, not knowing why, and read,

'To my beloved Paul on the eve of our wedding. Sally.'

Lexa's hands began to tremble, so affected was she by the poignancy of the words. She ought not to have looked; this was not for the eyes of strangers. It was like sacrilege to touch it, even with the reverence which she—— Suddenly her nerves went taut as a sound caught her ears. She swung round, tensed, alert, pulse racing. The door had opened almost soundlessly and Paul stood there, a tall menacing figure, gaunt, overpowering.

'Mr Mansell—I—I——' Her voice faltered to a stop and she shrank back, her eyes dilating at the sheer savagery in his. They were on fire, scorching her; his face was twisted with fury, his lips viciously contorted. But worst of all was the scar—livid and revolting, with that uncontrollable nerve throbbing in his throat. God, is he going to murder me? she thought, a terrified hand creeping to her own throat as if already she could feel his long lean fingers crushing the life out of her.

'What the hell are you doing with that?' he snarled, striding across the room. 'You snooping, prying little——' Whatever word he had in mind was stemmed as, reaching out, he ordered her merely by a look to hand over the picture. He gazed down at it, motionless, silent, his dark eyes staring ... staring not at the photograph but beyond it to some far distant place where love was, and life and laughter. His very pose pierced Lexa's tender heart and compassion flooded through her whole mind and body, quenching her fear. She took a step to bring herself to him, a mechanical movement born of the desire to soothe his pain.

'Mr Mansell—forgive me. I wasn't prying, as—as you think, but only——'

'You tampered with the lock!' The savage vibrancy of his voice echoed round the room even after he had finished speaking.

'No-no—I d-didn't!' she denied swiftly. 'It wasn't locked. You obviously thought it was, but when I came the other day——'

'The other day?'

'I came because of——' She stopped, suddenly aware that she might get Maria into trouble if she were to tell him how she came to be in his room in the first place. He might sack the girl. Even if he didn't she would of a surety experience the lash of his fury. Lexa's body sagged as she admitted the impossibility of explaining. She looked at him through eyes that were misty, and dark with misery and regret. 'I can only say I'm sorry, and—and leave it at that.'

His eyes had lost their fire as, narrowing, they subjected her to a contemptuous stare.

'It was merely a woman's curiosity, was it? It was strange, but I've always had the impression that you wanted to know what Alacho's mother was like.'

She nodded, not looking at him as she said,

'I admit it. But it wasn't as you suppose. I never meant to snoop, as you called it. I wish with all my heart I could explain.' Her eyes pleaded for understanding and yet she knew he could never understand, nor did she blame him. She had transgressed as far as he was concerned, invaded his privacy, and there was neither excuse nor forgiveness.

'There's no explanation other than the one I've mentioned.' He had calmed down, much to her relief, and yet the pain revealed in his eyes was even worse than his fury. 'I don't want you here,' he said dully. 'Pack your things and go.'

'Go. . . ?' She stared disbelievingly. Strange, but she had not contemplated a reaction such as this. Was he serious? Somehow she felt he had spoken on the spur of the moment.

'Alacho,' she said. 'What will she do?'

'Manage!' The word was a snarl of sheer hate, and for one terribly anxious second she thought that in his fury he would inadvertently crush the precious photograph to pulp. But she need not have worried; he held it with reverent fingers, touching the lovely hair before, turning to the open drawer, he put it back in the very same place from which Lexa had taken it only a few moments ago.

'Won't you let me stay with her until you've found another nanny?' she pleaded as he turned to face her again. 'I hope you will, Mr Mansell, for the child's sake only, not for mine.'

The thin lips curved in a sneer.

'You care so much for her, don't you?'

'She's a lovable little girl, and she needs her father desperately. I love her, but I'm no substitute for her own flesh and blood.' She was calm now, in full command of herself, and as she saw him again as he was a moment ago with that photograph, she found herself saying forcefully, uncaring whether or not she aroused his fury again, 'Your wife—Alacho's mother—would she want you to treat her baby in the way you have? Would she be happy knowing that you hate her, blame her for what happened? No, Mr Mansell, she would not!' The strength of her emotion drove her now and she said things which she knew she had wanted to say for weeks, and even months ago. 'Would your wife want you to neglect the living while you worshipped at the shrine of the dead——'

'Stop!' he snarled, taking a stride towards her. 'Don't you dare speak of my wife! Be quiet, I say! Be quiet!' The voice was raised so loud that Lexa feared it must be heard downstairs by the servants. But the next moment, to her horror, Paul put his head in his hands and she stood there, impotently watching his shoulders heave and shudder as he became utterly drowned in the throes of mental agony. Tears streamed down Lexa's face as she cursed herself for her action in coming here to take a look at the photograph. She moved on legs that felt like jelly, and silently left the room, making sure to close the door because she could not bear for any of the servants to come up and look in, not while Paul was like that.

Although she could not have felt less like going out, Lexa knew she could not bear to stay in. She would only pace about in her room, scourging herself for what she had done. The evidence of tears could not altogether be erased even though she bathed her eyes several times. Jeremy, bright and breezy as he greeted her, was soon asking gravely what was the matter.

'You've been crying. It's something serious?'

'I don't know——' She stopped and turned to him. 'Please don't ask me any questions, Jeremy. I shan't answer them anyway.'

He went silent for a space and when presently he spoke again his voice sounded almost cold.

'I'm sorry, I was only trying to be helpful. Perhaps you'd rather go back home?'

She shook her head, anxious that he should not leave her.

'I feel dreadfully depressed, so do bear with me. Let's go to the café.'

'If that's what you want.' He began to walk away and she fell into step beside him.

'Perhaps,' she faltered after a while, 'I won't be very good company.'

'You don't want to go to the café, then?'

Her mouth went tight. He had not known her long enough to take an attitude like this!

'No, I don't. I'll go back. You needn't come with me.' To her dismay she started to cry and before she knew it she was being held close to him in the shadows of the palms, his soothing voice trying to calm her, one hand stroking her hair.

'Don't cry so, my love. Tell me what's wrong.'

My love.... Lexa stiffened in his arms and tried to draw away, but he held her tightly against him. And without doubt there was a strange comfort in the warmth and nearness of his body, in the touch of his hand on her hair, in the knowledge that he cared something about her. A sigh that was almost a sob escaped her, but she leant against him, relaxing her body, sapping at his strength as she clung to him. And in the intimacy of the moment he bent his head and kissed her, but within seconds lifted his head again, and then pushed her from him.

'What. . . ?' Her voice faded to silence as her eyes followed the tall, swiftly-striding figure of the man who had gone past them.

'It's Paul,' she faltered. 'Mr Mansell.'

'Your boss?'

'Alacho's father. He—he saw me—us. . . ?' She asked the question even while knowing the answer.

'He seemed to stop, in fact—— Well, to hesitate.' Jeremy shrugged his shoulders. 'Does it matter? I expect he knows you'll get yourself a young man one day.'

Lexa pulled right away, and turned her back on him, anger and indignation, belated and unreasonable, sweeping over her.

'You ought not to have kissed me!' she cried. 'Oh, I wish he hadn't seen us!'

He looked at her, saying curiously,

'Is there some particular reason why he shouldn't have seen us?'

'I—you——' Her lips quivered. 'Not really,' she had to admit, 'but it didn't seem right.' Not after what had happened earlier, when she had expressed sincere remorse at taking the photograph from the drawer to look at it. Somehow, to come out here and let Jeremy hold her and kiss her seemed so very wrong, yet Lexa could not for the life of her have explained why. 'I just wish he hadn't seen us, that's all,' she added lamely.

'We kissed last night,' he reminded her, 'and the night before.'

'That was different. No one saw us.'

'Lexa dear, there isn't a reason in the world why you shouldn't be here with me, now is there?'

She shook her head.

'I suppose not,' she agreed, her eyes seeking Paul's

figure along the beach, but it had melded with the shadows and was lost to view.

'If he has any sense at all he'll know that an attractive girl like you is bound to have admirers. Nor would he expect you to turn down an offer of marriage if the right man came along.' A small pause and then, 'Would you turn down an offer if the right man came along, Lexa?' Something in the way he said that forced her to say,

'The right man hasn't come along, Jeremy, so there's no sense in my considering the question, is there?'

He said nothing for a space. Lexa felt a coldness about him and sighed. She wished she knew what she wanted. She had been happy with Jeremy, had looked forward each evening to seeing him, and yet there was this feeling of uncertainty regarding what she wanted from him. She had encouraged him, allowing him to kiss her, talking for hours about herself, listening for hours to him when he talked about himself. They had held hands when strolling along the beach, had sat close and intimate in the café....

She supposed she still considered him to be going too fast for her, felt she was being coerced—in some subtle way—into reciprocation. Perhaps if she had had other companions, a friend or two on the island, she would not have so readily come as close to Jeremy as she had—certainly not in such a short time.

'Are we going to the café, Lexa?' Jeremy took her hand in his as he spoke. 'There *is* something the matter, isn't there?' he added before she could answer him.

'There is,' she admitted, but added that it was nothing she could talk about.

'Very well.' That coolness was evident again, but he kept her hand in his. 'Is it to be the café?'

'Yes,' she assented after a pause. 'It might be best if we go there.'

'Best?' with a dry inflection. 'Are you afraid I might make love to you if we stay out here?'

'You wouldn't make love to me unless I agreed! And it so happens that I'm not in a very agreeable mood!'

'Good God, Lexa—what the devil's the matter with you?'

'I'm sorry. You shouldn't say things like that. I don't like it.'

'Old-fashioned? Well, I love you for it,' he owned, although a trifle sullenly. 'I've not met one of your kind before. It's refreshing but it leaves me at a loss—— What I mean is, I'm not quite sure how I ought to act.'

She glanced sideways at him.

'Just act naturally,' she said. 'Don't take anything for granted.'

'Are we quarrelling?' he wanted to know, a trace of amusement in the words.

'We haven't known one another long enough to quarrel,' she retorted shortly, and wondered why he laughed. However, his voice was serious as he said,

'We mustn't quarrel, Lexa dear. I like you a lot and I believe you're beginning to like me——' He stopped beneath a tall swaying coconut palm and put a finger under her chin, lifting her face and looking rather anxiously into it. 'Am I being too optimistic when I say you're beginning to care?'

She pushed his hand away, but gently.

'Jeremy, we've known one another for less than four days!'

'I asked you before—what has time to do with it?'

'And my reply was that you have to get to know one another.' She began to walk on, her thoughts racing back to that scene, and to that final moment when Paul put his head in his hands and his shoulders shook. And she knew she would have been more content to be with him.

talking to him, trying to give him some small degree of comfort. It was a revelation, this knowledge, but she did not think to probe further into the workings of her mind, or to ask herself why she preferred to be with Paul. Nor, strangely, did the question of her dismissal enter into her consciousness. It was forgotten!

'We have another three and a half weeks,' Jeremy was saying as he walked beside her along the beach towards the twinkling lights of the town at the end. 'It's a pity you don't have time off. It's usual, surely, for any employee to have at least one day a week off?'

'Not with a nanny. Who would look after Alacho if I were to insist on taking a day off?'

'You worry too much over her,' he said.

'She's been lonely——' Lexa stopped, vexed with herself for there seemed to be a slight on Paul in her words.

'How old was she when her mother died?' They were nearing the end of the beach and something made Lexa glance back to where the pearly lights of Paul's house flickered in the distance. The whole landscape was crystal clear in the moonlight, an enchanted realm of silver splendour beneath a diamond-filled tropical sky.

'She was one year old.' Her answer came belatedly. She did not want to talk about Alacho or her father, not to Jeremy. But when they were at last in the café, drinking delicious coffee and eating local pastries, he broached the subject again, asking Lexa if she knew the circumstances of Mrs Mansell's death.

'She must have been very young,' he added, 'to leave a one-year-old child.'

'Yes, I expect she was very young.'

'But you don't know how old?'

'No, I don't.'

'And her death,' he said again. 'What was it? Heart?'

Lexa hesitated, then resignedly told him that Alacho's mother had died in a fire.

'Mr Mansell has a dreadful scar on his face——'

'Mother told me about it. He got it ... in the fire?' Jeremy's face twisted. 'He and the child were saved, but his wife died?'

'He wasn't in the house at the time.' Lexa went on to explain what had happened, speaking reluctantly because she knew that Paul had never told any of his neighbours anything about himself. He scarcely ever spoke to them, in fact, and when he did it was merely to pass the time of day. Mrs Bardsley had said how curious everyone was, but that no one had ever been able to learn anything about the man who, almost five years ago, had bought the most beautiful house on the island from its million-aire owner, an American who was returning to his own country.

'God, how awful!' Jeremy's face was shadowed with pity. 'No wonder he's morose. Mother'll be very interested——'

'Jeremy,' broke in Lexa swiftly, 'I'd rather you kept this to yourself. I ought not to have told you about it, but you asked questions and I couldn't very well lie—when for instance you wanted to know how Mrs Mansell died. But Mr Mansell's reticent, likes to keep his affairs private. You won't say anything, will you?'

'No—not if you don't want me to.'

'Mr Mansell wouldn't be pleased if he knew I'd been discussing him with anyone.'

'I understand,' he returned soothingly.

'And can we now change the subject?'

He looked at her curiously, as he had looked at her earlier, when they were on the beach.

'You seem unable to talk freely about him,' he said.

'At times you're—well, touchy, sort of, if his name's mentioned—by me, that is.'

Yes, she secretly admitted, she was sometimes touchy when Jeremy spoke of her employer. Why was it? she wondered. There was no feasible answer to her question, and in any case, Jeremy, respecting her request, changed the subject, telling her that he and the rest of the family were going to Bangkok a week the following Monday on a sightseeing trip.

'Doreen—that's my sister—wants to stay for a week, but I'm not staying that long. I shall be away for only a couple of days. I can't waste a whole week away from you.'

She managed a smile, feeling guilty because she hadn't been very nice to him this evening.

'It's flattering to hear you say that, Jeremy.'

'It was meant as flattery, but it was sincere as well. I only wish there was some way that you could come with us or, better still, with me alone.' He paused, looking at her. 'You were telling me you'd taken Alacho to Bangkok on a visit. Can't you do the same again?'

She shook her head.

'I don't think so, Jeremy. You see, on that occasion Alacho wanted to see her father, and that was the reason I took her.'

'Wanted to see him?' he said, diverted. 'What for?'

'I'd rather not say.'

'Touchy again, eh?'

'I asked you not to talk about Alacho's father.'

'It was you who mentioned him,' he reminded her. And, when she did not speak, 'It's plain now why he hasn't any time for the child——' He stopped. 'Sorry, Lexa. I ought to keep my thoughts and conclusions to myself. To get back to this idea of you and me having a trip to Bangkok—I'm sure you could wangle something if you gave your mind to it. Bring Alacho. I shan't be over-joyed, but I won't grumble. On the contrary,' he added swiftly, seeing Lexa lift her brows, 'I shall be grateful for small mercies.'

To her own surprise Lexa heard herself say,

'I'll see what can be done. We'll be staying at the Ayudhya Palace, if we do come. Mr Mansell owns it—but you probably know?'

'Yes, Mother was mentioning it the other day as a matter of fact. He owns several hotels in Bangkok, I understand?'

'And some in Pattaya.'

'Rich man!'

'I suppose he is.'

'We're on the forbidden subject again. Come on, Lexa,' he added after a pause, 'let's go.'

They walked back along the beach, under the moon, and as he left her at her gate he put his arms around her waist and drew her to him. His lips were warm and ten-der, his arms about her comforting. She thought as she got into bed later: he's nice and he'd ask me to marry him if I wanted him to—even now, after only a few days.

She pulled up the cover, turning her face into the pil-low. Her thoughts had switched to Paul and she won-dered what he was doing at this moment. Looking at the photograph? Living in the past when the world was bright, the future a vision of roses and red wine?

Lexa swallowed the pain in her throat but had no power to quell the scalding tears that filled her eyes. Little had she known, when she had accepted the post offered by a man she disliked intensely, that his sorrow would affect her emotions as profoundly as this.

CHAPTER SIX

WHATEVER the reason for his visit, Paul went off the following morning early, and Lexa made no mention to Alacho of his having been home. She wondered if she would hear any more about her dismissal and rather thought that her confidence in the security of her post had not been misplaced. Would Paul ask her to stay, or would he simply forget it, convinced that she would do the same?

All day Lexa felt restless, and Alacho's mood did nothing to help. The child was fractious, pouting over her lessons, pretending she could not do her sums, and even complaining about the food she had for lunch.

'I've had just about enough of you today!' Lexa told her severely. 'Do you want to spend the rest of it in your bedroom?'

'No! But I don't like this meat!'

'Then leave it.'

'I don't like the vegetables, either.'

Lexa took the plate away and put a custard tart before her.

'Ugh! I can't eat that!'

Exasperated, Lexa could almost have smacked her. It wasn't as if there was anything wrong healthwise; Alacho was as fit as ever, her colour normal.

'I think perhaps you're tired,' she said. 'An hour or two in bed'll do you more good than going to the beach.' In fact, Lexa would have welcomed a couple of hours' rest herself, as she had slept fitfully, the picture of Paul ever before her consciousness during the wakeful periods.

'I shan't go to sleep!'

'Alacho, don't speak to me in that tone of voice. Just what's wrong with you?'

'I want my daddy to be here all the time!'

So that was it! Tears stood out on Alacho's lashes and Lexa, filled with remorse, got up and went to the other side of the table, slipping an arm around her shoulders.

'He'll be home soon, love. He can't be here all the time, you know that.'

'Then why can't we go and live in Bangkok?'

'In the hotel? You wouldn't like that all the time.'

'Daddy could buy a house, and then we could all live together in it. We could come here for holidays like some other people do.'

'It isn't possible, Alacho.'

'I'm fed up, Lexa,' cried Alacho pettishly. 'What can we do this afternoon?'

'Go into town if you like?'

They went immediately after lunch and the first person they saw when they went into the stationery shop was Jeremy.

'Hello!' eagerly from Alacho. 'What are you buying?'

'A card for Stella.' He looked down into the lovely face, then up to meet Lexa's eyes. 'A beauty,' he said, then added, 'She'll break some hearts in a few years from now.'

Lexa frowned. She had no wish to contemplate a future so far ahead.

'Let her enjoy her childhood first. With maturity come the problems.'

He said with an odd inflection,

'You have problems?'

'Everyone has problems.'

'Mr——' Alacho stopped, tilting her head enquiringly. 'Shall I call you Jeremy? Stella does.'

'If you like.'

'Jeremy, will you come with us to have a drink and a cake?'

'Of course,' he laughed. 'I thought you'd never ask me!'

He bought the card, while Lexa purchased some notepaper and envelopes, and a colouring book for Alacho.

'The tea-shop's in that street—' Alacho pointed and then added excitedly, 'There's Mrs Bardsley and the children! Will they come as well?'

'I expect so.'

The children had seen them and soon they were all trooping into the café where they occupied one of the largest tables, on a sort of dais with a piano at one end of it.

Lexa had not had much to do with Paul's nearest neighbour, but on the rare occasions when she had stopped for a chat she had enjoyed the company. The old lady was witty, with a way of emphasising words that ought not to be emphasised at all, yet for all that there was something attractive in the way she spoke. She was about sixty-eight, with thick iron-grey hair and twinkling grey-green eyes. Her clothes were smart but a little old-fashioned. She had been in her late thirties when she got married. Doreen had come along a year later, but she was forty-two when Jeremy was born. This had come from Jeremy, when he was telling Lexa all about himself.

'How very *nice* to see you, Lexa. Jeremy's been *telling* me about your growing friendship! You've *certainly* made an impression on him, which is something to your credit, I can tell you!'

Lexa coloured and smiled. Alacho was talking excitedly to the three girls, while the boy, Billy, sat listening and looking rather out of it all. Lexa spoke to him and, used as she was to young children, soon brought him out of his silence. Jeremy watched her all the time; he seemed unable to take his eyes off her, so much so that she began to feel embarrassed.

'You certainly have a way with children,' he whispered at a moment when his mother and the youngsters were busy munching cakes and chattering at the same time. 'You're rather wonderful, you know.'

'Thank you.' She was shy, and uneasy; his deep interest troubled her.

'Are you having some more tea, Lexa?' Mrs Bardsley had the pot poised and Lexa nodded, passing her cup along the table.

'I wish Tuesday would come quicker!' Stella laughed as she spoke and added, 'Gran says I won't be wanting birthdays when I'm as old as she is, but I'm sure I will! I love getting up in the morning of my birthday and knowing I'm having lots and lots of presents!'

'I've got a nice present for you,' put in Alacho happily, 'but I can't tell you what it is because it wouldn't be a surprise. But I've got one and you like it and its colour's wh——'

'Alacho!' exclaimed Lexa, laughing. 'Just hold your tongue——' She put up a warning finger. 'Hold it, I said!'

Everybody laughed, and quite naturally others in the café looked and laughed as well. And just at that moment Lexa glanced up, to where the more select and expensive part of the café was situated, on a balcony hung with flowers and a jade vine. She started visibly as her eyes met those of her employer. So he hadn't gone back to the city after all. . . . He had merely come into town. A shiver ran along her spine as she realised what had happened. He had not slept, had risen early and come into town, staying here, wandering about, lonely, unhappy, trying to find peace of mind.

She wondered if he had always been like this, and just could not accept that he had, not for five enduring years. No, impossible, since he would have become unbalanced long before now.

Something had happened recently; Lexa seemed to *know*, almost as if she had been given the idea by some intuitive impression whose action had been slightly delayed. Yes, something had happened recently ... but what ...?

She stole another glance, saw the grey eyes move to Jeremy, where they remained for one inscrutable moment before flickering to the happy, laughing face of his daughter ... and the bitterness that came to his expression was terrible to see ... and it was sheer undiluted pain in Lexa's heart....

The day of the party began with Alacho catapulting into Lexa's bedroom before she was up and demanding to know how long it would be before she could put on her party dress.

'Hours and hours yet.'

The excitement went on all morning, with Alacho quite unable to concentrate on her lessons.

'How long now?' she had asked every half hour or so.

'Get on with your writing.'

'Do you think Stella will like her present? I told you how she liked my white shoulder bag when I showed it her and she said she wished she had one the same, so I bought one—I mean,' amended Alacho with a grin, '*you* bought one. I wanted to tell her what her present was when we were in the café, but I didn't——'

'You almost did,' interrupted Lexa dryly, 'by describing it.'

A laugh rang out.

'I wanted her to be guessing!'

'Well, she wouldn't have been guessing. She'd have guessed!'

'How long is it now?'

'Alacho,' said Lexa sternly, 'get on with your writing.'

'It's hard to think of the words when I'm thinking of the party.'

'If you don't do as you're told you won't be going to the party!'

'Ooh ... you wouldn't do that to me, Lexa! I'd cry all afternoon, and I wouldn't eat anything. You call it hunger strike. I know because one of my other nannies said so——'

'Are you going to do that writing?' The soft quality in Lexa's voice, the stern enquiry which carried a distinct note of warning ... these had their effect and Alacho put her head down at last. Lexa was looking through her 'daily diary' when she became aware of Alacho's attention straying even yet again.

'It's Daddy!' she exclaimed excitedly, her eyes on the window. 'He's come home again already, and he only went away yesterday! Oh, I'm glad! Will he stay for a little while, do you think?'

'I hope so, dear.' Lexa laid aside the child's workbook and rose to her feet as, taking a short cut across the lawn, her employer came to the verandah of the classroom and entered it, a small suitcase in his hand. He had obviously come up from the boat by taxi, thought Lexa, waiting with a slight tremor of apprehension for him to speak. She had not seen him to speak to since that exchange of glances in the café and now she quite naturally wondered if he was intending to mention her dismissal—to ask, perhaps, if she had made arangements for her journey back to England.

She thought too of his unexpected arrival on that fateful evening when he had found her in his room; Maria had told her later that he did sometimes come home without phoning first. It was just as the mood took him, Maria had said casually. Lexa thought it strange indeed—his coming so soon after he had sent for his clothes and could only surmise that some change of plan had occurred. However, it had nothing to do with her and she had dismissed the matter from her mind.

'Miss Duke,' he was saying, after having spoken briefly to his daughter, 'I want to speak to you, now. Come along to my study.' He seemed anxious, she thought, as he added briefly, 'It's important.'

'But Alacho——'

'Will stay quiet and continue with whatever she's doing.' He turned to her. 'Don't move. Understand?'

'Yes, Daddy.' The child's lips trembled at the way he spoke to her and Lexa frowned. She had been so excited to see him arrive. But then it was always the same: the child was eager for him to be here, yet when he was he gave her scant attention. Perhaps now and then he would talk to her, ask how she was getting on with her lessons. It escaped his notice entirely that Alacho lapped it up avidly and craved for more.

He had left the room even before Lexa moved from the desk, and was in his study when she went in, standing by the window, so incredibly tall! So formidable, with all his arrogant dignity intact—strengthened, she thought, because of his weakness the other evening when he had seemed to be weeping ... no, not merely weeping but sobbing piteously. But Lexa rather thought that it was merely an impression she had gained, that tears would never be shed by a man like Paul. Such lack of control would be even worse than the lack he had already displayed a few minutes earlier, when he had allowed his fury to get the better of him.

Lexa stood just inside the door, looking at him, waiting for him to speak first, his expression strengthening her previous impression that he was anxious.

The silence was broken at last, a sort of electric silence that affected them both in a way neither could understand.

'Sit down,' he invited brusquely, indicating a chair. She did as she was told, leaning back against the upholstery, making an effort to retain her calm, which she did, much to her own surprise, and she actually found herself saying, with the idea of forestalling him,

'I expect you're going to ask if I'm ready to leave?' So unemotional! But she was *not* ready to leave, since she could not visualise what Alacho's life would be like without her. It would be cruelty itself to deny her the only love she had ever consciously known, and Lexa felt that she would even humble herself and ask that her services be retained.

Paul was looking at her, his face inscrutable in the shadows cast by a dhak tree, whose flowers of brilliant crimson were swaying gently outside the window.

'I am not going to ask if you're ready to leave, Miss Duke,' he said after a pause that stretched uncomfortably. 'On the contrary, I'm asking you to stay.'

She nodded mechanically, aware that this was what she had half expected, so she was not in the least taken by surprise at his request. She saw the position from his point of view: she was here, doing her job efficiently;

Alacho liked her—no, loved her—so was happy and obedient. To make a drastic change could produce havoc, for Alacho, despite her charming ways, could be wilful and awkward. Paul had no time or patience for her, so as far as he was concerned it was infinitely more sensible to leave things as they were. As Lexa had surmised from the first, her job was safe. Her dismissal the other evening was given her on the spur of the moment, when he was torn both by anger and grief.

'I'll stay,' she told him quietly. 'And——' She stopped and looked at him for a moment as if debating the wisdom of voicing her next words. He was looking questioningly at her, so she continued. 'I want to apologise for my behaviour the other evening, Mr Mansell. I bitterly regret it, please believe me.' Her voice caught, all unknowingly, and her beautiful eyes were shadowed. He looked and frowned and glanced away. And to her amazement his own voice was not quite steady when at length he spoke.

'We'll forget it, Miss Duke. I don't expect it will occur again.'

'I don't think you can ever forget it,' she murmured regretfully.

'I do realise that I was mistaken when I accused you of tampering with the lock. I saw afterwards that I'd omitted to lock the drawer.'

It was an awkward conversation and Lexa ended it by saying that she would have to go as Alacho was going to a party later and she had to have an early lunch so that she would have plenty of time to get ready.

'Mrs Bardsley wants the party to begin early—about two o'clock, because there are games to play first.'

'The Bardsleys. . . .' He was regarding her thoughtfully. 'The young man you were with on the beach—he's a visitor there, I believe?'

'He's their son.' If only she could say more—tell him that what he saw was meaningless, that she had no intention of going out with Jeremy again.

'Ah, yes, I seem to remember hearing from somewhere that they had a son in England and a married daughter with several children. I saw some strange children on the beach. I presume they are the Bardsleys' grandchildren on a visit?'

'Yes, and it's one of them—Stella—who's having the birthday party.'

'Has Alacho a suitable dress?' asked Paul, surprising her.

'Yes; we bought one in town.'

'We?' frowningly.

'I bought it, but please don't offer me the money. I bought it as a present.'

Paul was shaking his head.

'Let me have the bill. I won't have anyone paying for such things out of their own salaries.'

She shrugged.

'I'd have liked to have bought it,' she said.

'So it's settled that you stay?' He looked at her, ignoring her last words.

'Yes, of course.'

'Perhaps,' he said as she rose from the chair, 'I shall consider sending Alacho to boarding-school, probably within the next year.'

Lexa swallowed, and said in response to an inner prompting,

'You don't really believe she'll be happy at boarding-school, Mr Mansell.'

His eyes narrowed.

'She'll get by.'

'Surely you care?'

'You know very well that I don't.'

He was callous! How she came to waste her pity on such a man was utterly beyond her comprehension.

'I'd better go,' she said stiffly, and then, turning at the door, 'Shall you be staying until Sunday afternoon?'

'I'm home for a fortnight. I'll be having a guest for part of the time, an Englishwoman. You'll have company.' His voice was harsh, his eyes like metal. What was he thinking to make him scowl? wondered Lexa, feeling that, as long as he *was* having a guest, he ought to be looking a little happier about it. For she knew who the visitor was ... the woman she had seen him with in the hotel. Nevertheless, she heard herself say,

'An Englishwoman, Mr Mansell?'

'Mrs Sharman—Evelyn Sharman.' Again that harsh edge to his voice, but at the same time there was the most odd expression in his eyes as he looked searchingly into Lexa's. It was as if an idea had come to him and he was rather stunned by it.

'She's married, then?' Lexa's voice was easier and she realised it had been strained before. Why should she care whether Mrs Sharman was married or not?

'She's a divorcee.'

'Oh. . . .' Lexa could not have described her feelings at this moment. All she knew was that a dryness had come to her throat, and that there was a dragging sensation in her heart. Paul was staring at her and, disconcerted, she glanced away. From somewhere in the garden came the sweet lilting call of a bird, drifting through the silence of the room.

'If there's nothing else I'll go.' She glanced at him as she spoke, noticing the stony eyes, devoid of expression. He was distant, withdrawn into himself and she wondered if he had forgotten her presence altogether. She went from the room and was sure he had not noticed her leave. Alacho was nibbling the end of her pencil when she got back to her and with a smile she told her to stop work.

'It's time you had a bit of lunch and then got ready,' she added.

'What did Daddy want you for?' Alacho put down her pencil and came over to the desk. 'Was he angry?'

Lexa shook her head, managing to produce a reassuring smile.

'No, darling, he wasn't angry. Pass me your book and let me see what you've done.'

'I think it's very good.' Alacho ran back to her place and brought the book. 'But please leave it, Lexa,' she said impatiently. 'I want to put my new dress on!'

'Lunch first, my pet.'

'But I won't be able to eat anything at the party!'

'Of course you will. In any case, the actual party's not until about four o'clock. You'd be starving by that time.'

She was glancing at what Alacho had done. It was excellent work for a six-year-old—imaginative writing illustrated with charming little drawings. Lexa decided on impulse to show it to her father. Meanwhile, however, she gave Alacho her lunch, having a snack with her. Then came the exciting interlude of getting ready, with Alacho scarcely able to stand still.

'Ooh.... You're tugging my hair!'

'Then for goodness' sake keep still!'

'Isn't my frock lovely? Shall I show it to Daddy?' The animation had lessened, the brightness of the eyes faded a little. 'He never looks at what I'm wearing.'

'We'll let him see this pretty dress, though.' Lexa felt she might be snubbed, told not to trouble him, but on the other hand Paul might just be in the mood to pass some flattering comment to his lovely daughter. And she *was* lovely, like a doll in her frilly dress, short—very short—in a most delicate colour described by the shop assistant as Whisper Green. The bodice was ruched, the skirt very full, with tiny frills from waist to hem, a Peter Pan collar and ribbons falling from the front, ribbons in several shades of green. Alacho's shoes and socks were white, as was the ribbon in her curls. Lexa had made a pretty parcel of the shoulder bag and Alacho insisted on taking this with her when eventually Lexa took her to find her father. He was not in the saloon, nor was there any response when Lexa knocked on his study door.

He was in the garden, relaxing—much to Lexa's surprise because she had never seen him really relaxed before—in a brightly-upholstered lounger, a book on the grass by his side. He was staring into space, but sat up and looked when they came into view.

'Daddy——' Alacho ran to him, her face anxious and yet expectant too. 'Do you like my beautiful dress? It's a party dress and it's the nicest one I've ever had!'

She stood, her eyes pleading, her mouth quivering. Lexa felt that if Paul did not pander to the child's obvious desire she would come back and tell him what she thought about him. But her heart warmed even as the resolve was made, for his eyes had softened miraculously, and his voice held only admiration as he said,

'I certainly do like your beautiful dress, Alacho. And it suits you to perfection. What colour do you call it? I don't think I've ever noticed a shade like that before.'

Alacho was silent, dazed, her big eyes disbelieving. It was a poignant moment and Lexa felt like an intruder, felt that if only she were not present Paul might have gone as far, even, as to show his daughter some affection.

If only he would kiss her! Had he ever done so? Yes, Lexa was sure of it, sure that when she was tiny he had loved her dearly, for how could it be otherwise, when he had adored her mother so?

'The—the colour is—is Whisper Green, Daddy.' The trembling childish voice was heard at last, and to Lexa's further amazement Paul held out both hands and told Alacho to come to him. She dropped the parcel on the grass and advanced slowly, almost awkwardly as if she were doing something for the very first time.

'What have you got in that pretty parcel?' he asked when she had put her tiny hands in his. 'Obviously it's a present for—Stella?' He looked at Lexa, but she let Alacho answer.

'Yes, that's right. Stella's the middle one—— Well, there isn't a middle one really because there are four children, but she's between Emma and Janie. The other one's a boy and his name is Billy.' She smiled, her confidence growing all the time. 'It's a shoulder bag like mine—you know, the one I nearly always use because I like it best. It's white.'

Paul's face was a study. He knew nothing about any bag his daughter owned, white or otherwise, but he said gently,

'Ah, that one. Yes, it's attractive and useful. Stella's going to be delighted with her present, I'm sure.'

He seemed to stop speaking rather abruptly, his eyes flickering towards Lexa, who had the impression that he had astounded himself as much as he had astounded both his daughter and her nanny.

He became distant, his face taut. With swift understanding Lexa whisked her charge away before he could say or do anything to shatter the pleasure he had just given to his child.

'We'll have to go. Mrs Bardsley said the games would be starting at two o'clock.'

'Goodbye, Daddy. I'll tell you all about it when I come home!' And before either Lexa or Paul could guess at her intention Alacho had kissed her father on the lips.

CHAPTER SEVEN

HE said to Lexa three days later,

'What are you trying to do, Miss Duke?'

She answered without hesitation, fully aware of what he meant.

'I'm trying to bring you and Alacho together.'

They were on the verandah, Paul having come upon her as he emerged from his study. It was evening and Alacho was in bed. Lexa intended taking a stroll along the beach, but later, when she would be meeting Jeremy after he had dined with his family.

'You're not adopting a very subtle approach.' Paul surprised her by sitting down, his expression unfathomable in the soft glow from lights hidden in the foliage of a jade vine. Its flowers had bloomed abundantly in February and March, their turned-up petals pale jade in colour. Now, however, all was foliage—large, exquisitely-shaped leaves hanging from a trellis interwoven to form a roof over the verandah.

'I did think of it,' was Lexa's frank rejoinder, 'but I soon accepted that you would see through any manoeuvre.'

The hint of a smile touched the fine outline of his mouth. He had been different since the occasion when Alacho had shown him her dress, not dramatically different, it was true, but there certainly was some fine shade of change in his attitude towards his daughter. Lexa had shown him Alacho's work, watching his face closely to catch any fleeting hint of pride ... and she did not watch in vain! A sense of triumph had sent her spirits soaring and even the depressing knowledge that Mrs Sharman was to arrive at the week-end was overshadowed by the pure joy she derived from that look on her employer's face.

'You're very frank,' commented Paul, leaning back and hitching up a trouser leg, an action that made him seem more human, more natural than ever before. 'I seem to remember remarking once before on your honesty.' A strange inflection in his voice, some trace of censure beneath the words he spoke ... and Lexa's eyes flew to his in swift interrogation. His lids came down and his hand reached for the bell-rope dangling from a pillar close to where he sat.

'I rather think,' said Lexa, glancing away again, 'that frankness is what you would always demand. And I suppose honesty is the same thing.'

The grey eyes were inscrutable but not hard, the voice clipped, censorious but by no means hostile.

'I asked you to be honest with me at all times, Miss Duke.'

Lexa looked at him and said bewilderedly,

'I have been honest—I don't know what you're trying to say, Mr Mansell.'

The grey eyes were challenging.

'You haven't always been frank with me,' he reproved. 'I'm talking now about the occasion when you were in my bedroom.' He was calm, incredibly so, as he mentioned the scene of that most dramatic incident, while Lexa on the other hand was blushing with embarrassment, relieved when a servant arrived and Paul's attention was diverted as he ordered a pot of coffee to be brought out to the verandah.

'For two, sir?' said the manservant respectfully, his glance flickering to Lexa.

'Yes, for two.'

The man went away and Paul spoke immediately, telling Lexa that Maria had let it out that she had asked her to look in his room for the missing items of clothing.

'You'd obviously opened the drawer and seen the photograph before that evening when I came in,' he said finally.

'That's so,' she said with difficulty. 'But on that occasion I was able to resist temptation, and I closed the drawer at once—when I noticed the photograph, that was.'

'Conscience?' he asked briefly.

'Not exactly——' She paused in thought. 'Yes, I suppose you could call it that. I knew I had no right to be looking in that drawer at all.'

'You were searching, at Maria's request, for some clothes I wanted.'

'I know. But they couldn't possibly be in that drawer.' She looked at him apologetically. 'It was automatic—you know what I mean? I felt I must look everywhere.'

'And why, when you'd decided not to look at the photograph, did you later go back?'

'I suppose it originated—the desire, I mean—with Alacho. She's so lovely, has such adorable ways, and I've wondered several times what her mother was like.' Her eyes were still on his. It seemed strange to be talking about his wife in this matter-of-fact way after that terrible scene in the bedroom. Up till now he had not wanted to talk about her with Lexa—nor with anyone else, she suspected. It was his own secret, his private grief, and he had no wish to share any of it with another person.

'And the temptation got the better of you?'

She nodded, her eyes on his hands, sensitive hands,

long-fingered and brown. The scar showed below the whiteness of his shirt cuff, but it was nothing. And, strangely, neither was the scar on his face. Pale in the lamplight's glow, it was almost insignificant and she realised that only when his emotions were aroused did it become ugly—livid and raised up as if it were swollen.

'I felt it couldn't do anyone any harm,' she said, the hint of misery in her voice coming through so plainly that he was bound to catch it.

'Why didn't you explain?' he demanded, an edge of anger to his voice. 'You allowed me to think it was merely woman's morbid curiosity that had led you there.'

She looked steadily at him.

'You weren't in the mood for explanations,' she reminded him.

'Nevertheless, you were, at one moment, intending to explain,' Paul countered, and she nodded automatically.

'Yes, I was, but then it struck me that I might be getting Maria into trouble, because she ought not to have asked me to look for the clothes.'

'Why not? It was the natural thing to have someone else look, just to make absolutely sure.'

A deep sigh escaped her.

'I didn't know you'd take it like that, Mr Mansell.' She would have liked to add that he was so unpredictable that even now she was amazed by his manner.

'I try to be fair, Miss Duke, no matter what my other shortcomings are.' He turned as the manservant arrived with the tray. It was put on the table and Paul asked Lexa to pour the coffee.

She did as she was told, still dwelling on this new, tolerant attitude towards her, and feeling glad that he no longer believed her to have been prying, taking a liberty for no other reason than that she was morbidly curious about his wife.

'Mrs Sharman will be staying for a week,' he said later as they drank their coffee. 'She'll return to Bangkok when I leave, which will be a week on Monday.'

'She's merely having a holiday here, as your guest?'

He nodded, and she noticed—as once before when Mrs Sharman's visit was mentioned—the stony brilliance that lit his eyes. It was almost as if he was hating the idea of the girl's visit. Which was ridiculous, Lexa was soon telling herself, simply because it was by his own invitation that she was coming here.

He got up soon afterwards and left her; she remained for a short while, thoughtfully going over the conversation they had had. It had all begun with his asking what she was trying to do. Then it had veered and he had brought up the incident in the bedroom. Lexa would have liked to talk again about Alacho, and even to ask outright if he was beginning to have some affection for his child. Certainly there was this slight change, and, heartened by it, Lexa was more determined than ever to bring her plan to fruition.

Mrs Sharman duly arrived, bringing with her what to Lexa—who watched the unloading of the car from the balcony of her bedroom—seemed to be enough luggage to last a couple of months. Paul had not met the boat himself, but had sent the chauffeur. He came from the house as the car stopped and Lexa interestedly watched the way they greeted one another. No sign of affection, but at least Paul produced a smile. True, he had smiled on half a dozen occasions since she had known him, but always the smile had come slowly, reluctantly, and not on every occasion was it a smile at all, but merely a curve of his lips that could be read as cynical or sardonic, or even put in the category of a sneer. Now, though, the smile came easily, bringing a little gasp to

Lexa's lips. The attractiveness of him! Every nerve was affected, every pulse had quickened. What was the matter with her? This was not the first time she had been affected by Paul ... nor was it by any means the first time that the idea of his having this woman friend affected her in a way she could not understand.

Dejected, she turned away and went out to the back garden where Alacho was playing with the dog, chasing him all over the lawn one moment while he was chasing her the next. Her laughter rang out; it was what Lexa needed to cheer her up.

'Come and play with us,' called Alacho between her laughter. 'It's great fun!'

The dog, a brown and white mongrel the size of a fox-terrier, was enjoying the game as much as the child. Lexa stood watching, saying she was not quite up to running about just at present.

After a while she became conscious of someone watching her and she turned. Mrs Sharman was at an upstairs window, looking out. Their eyes met, only briefly, but there was a cold, brittle quality in Evelyn Sharman's that actually brought a frown to Lexa's forehead. She had not cared for the woman before; she disliked her intensely now.

Only seconds later Lexa was chiding herself. Just because the woman was a friend of Paul it did not mean that she had to dislike her. She had never even spoken to her, so this attitude was not only absurd but it was bitchy!

'Lexa, come on!' Alacho's voice again, ringing through the scented garden. The sun was beginning to fall and everything was bathed in a golden light. The rose beds were deeper scarlet because of it, the yellow dripping candle-bush was darker too. Shadows already pervaded the outer rim of the grounds where tall palms towered over the tropical vegetation below. All was peaceful, all was silent around the child and dog, with the only movement being the slight wash on the shore where the waves gently caressed it.

'I think it's time you were coming in for your tea, Alacho.' Lexa went slowly towards her, watching that the dog did not decide to jump up at her. But he sat on his haunches, mouth wide, tongue hanging.

'I've tired him out!' laughed Alacho, delighted. 'And he's got four legs! He ought to be able to run twice as far as me!'

'It doesn't work quite like that,' said Lexa in some amusement. 'Poor Pango, he wants a drink badly.'

'I'll go and get him one, then, from the kitchen!'

She was a long time gone; Lexa bent to stroke the dog for a while and was just deciding to go and see what was keeping her when she appeared, without the water, but trotting by her father's side. On his other side was Mrs Sharman, looking like the picture of a model in *Vogue* or some other glossy magazine. Her dress was so smoothly fitting that it might have been modelled on her svelte figure; her hair was immaculate, straight and gleaming, her make-up perfect—lips rouged, eyes shadowed very correctly, lashes mascaraed, brows shaped, hands that seemed never to have been soiled since the day they saw the light.

Paul introduced her to Lexa, his face devoid of expression. Impossible to guess at his feelings, or to sense any emotion whatsoever. The woman, however, was smiling as she held out a hand.

'I'm happy to meet you, Miss Duke. I think we saw one another a short while ago. I was looking through my bedroom window.' Lexa said nothing to this and the other woman went on, 'How are you liking Thailand? It must be a great change from what you've been used to?'

'Of course. Everything about it is new.'

'You like it, though?'

'Very much.' Her eyes slid to Paul. He seemed bored and Lexa made an excuse to get away, saying it was Alacho's tea time.

Evelyn Sharman had been at the house two days when Lexa found herself alone with her. She had been slightly troubled by Alacho's pallor from the moment she saw her getting out of bed. She had asked if she felt unwell and was quickly assured that she was all right. But breakfast was a silent meal, with Lexa's attempts at conversation being almost ignored. The result was that instead of lessons that morning it was back to bed for the child, Lexa staying with her until she went off to sleep.

Deciding to see her father at once, Lexa had looked for him in vain, and an enquiry in the kitchen brought from one of the maids the information that he had gone into town and would be away for about a couple of hours. Naturally anxious, Lexa had asked Maria about a doctor and was given a number. Further frustration was caused when the number was engaged, and although she tried several times the result was the same and she concluded that there was something wrong with the telephone system, which was not all that good at the best of times.

After glancing in to Alacho's room and ascertaining that she was sleeping peacefully Lexa went out into the garden, deciding to stroll around, for here she seemed always to find peace of mind, soothed by the sheer beauty and colour of the sun-drenched tropical aspect to be observed on every side. But to her disgust she came face to face with the woman she least wanted to see. A smile widened the painted lips, but there was no warmth in it; on the contrary, it was stiff and chill, matching the cold unfathomable depths of the large grey eyes.

'Aren't you in the schoolroom this morning, Miss Duke?' she asked unnecessarily, her voice purringly unpleasant to Lexa's critical ears. 'I'd find it so wretchedly boring, looking after a child all the time.' A pause, but Lexa was not inclined to speak and Evelyn went on, undaunted by the distant manner which Lexa adopted, 'Do you think you'll be able to endure it indefinitely—after having had such an interesting life in England?'

'There's no question of enduring it,' returned Lexa brusquely. 'I'm happy in my job, and I certainly can't foresee any changes in the near future.' A slight pause, but not long enough for the girl to speak. 'How do you know I had an interesting life in England?'

'Paul told me.' The girl's mouth went tight. 'He seemed anxious in case you decided to leave, but as I told him, there's always an alternative to having a nanny: he can send Alacho to boarding-school. She'd be better there, in the company of other children of her own age.'

'He has mentioned boarding-school,' said Lexa broodingly, 'and all I can hope is that he won't pursue the matter. Boarding-school isn't for Alacho—and I'm speaking from my experience of children, especially young ones. Besides, in my opinion father and daughter should be together. I'd like to see them close.' She glanced away, to where canna lilies and blanket flowers and dahlias flaunted their colour or foliage in the sunshine.

'In *your* opinion.' At the arrogance of Mrs Sharman's voice Lexa turned her head again. 'And who do you think you are to express an opinion, Miss Duke?'

Amazed, Lexa merely stared for a space, noticing the narrowed eyes and points of ice within them, the haughty set of the mouth and lift of the chin. Antagonism was there, undisguised, blatantly evident. But why? Lexa's expression was one of baffled enquiry as she said,

'I don't think I understand your attitude, Mrs Sharman. Have I said something to annoy you?' It was the schoolteacher speaking, exhibiting her practised diplomacy, suppressing a natural instinct to retaliate.

The question brought colour to the other woman's face; it was with a feeling of satisfaction that Lexa saw the embarrassment which replaced the cold hauteur on her face.

'No—er—no, you haven't exactly annoyed me, Miss Duke. But on the other hand, it did appear somewhat presumptuous of you to put your opinion into words.'

'Must I keep my opinions to myself? Is that what you mean?' There was a half-smile on Lexa's face; she meant to disconcert her antagonist even further if she could. 'Surely, as Alacho's nanny, I ought to be outright in my opinion regarding her well-being?'

'Well—yes, of course.' Mrs Sharman paused uncertainly, regarding Lexa with a hint of suspicion as if she did not quite know how to take her. 'But as regards her relationship with her father——' The woman stopped and frowned and then went on, 'You must have discovered that he has no love for her?'

Lexa stiffened, and her eyes were brittle suddenly. But her sense of tact remained unimpaired.

'Mrs Sharman,' she said gently, 'aren't you speaking out of turn? I'm only a servant, you know, and for that reason I'm not in a position to discuss my employer, either with you or anyone else.' That half-smile again and then, 'I'm sure you will agree with me, Mrs Sharman?'

The grey eyes regarded her with steely intent.

'You're a clever woman.' The words came slowly, unexpectedly. 'It's plain that you're practised in battles of words. Have you had so many?' Amusement replaced the metal in the woman's eyes. 'Paul told me you were an infant teacher for four years.'

'That's correct.' Lexa became restless, wanting to get back to the telephone and ring for the doctor. 'Please excuse me,' she said. 'I'm troubled about Alacho, and I want to have the doctor take a look at her——'

'She's ill?'

'Not exactly ill, but certainly not herself. I've put her to bed and she's sleeping quite peacefully—at least, she was when I left her a few minutes ago, but——'

'You're probably fussing too much,' interrupted Mrs Sharman on a note of indifference. 'Children *are* sometimes off colour, aren't they? But, like animals, they seem to right themselves if left alone.'

'Alacho won't be left alone; she'll have medical attention just as soon as I can get it.'

'It seems to me,' said Mrs Sharman, 'that the child is being outrageously pampered, Miss Duke.'

Lexa looked at her, wondering just how close was the relationship between this woman and Paul Mansell. It was no superficial one, she decided, because if it was then the woman would not be speaking with this arrogant confidence that was scraping like a rasp on Lexa's temper, so much so that she was beginning to have the greatest difficulty in holding it in check. Diplomacy was all right, but there was a limit beyond which it was often impossible to go.

'Alacho is not being pampered,' she retorted, 'but she is receiving the care which I'm being paid to give her.'

Mrs Sharman's teeth seemed to snap together, but before she had time to speak Paul's car came bowling smoothly along the drive, his chauffeur at the wheel. Paul had seen the girls, and as soon as the car stopped he got out and came towards them, his strides long and easy, his body swinging with the rhythm of an athlete taking leisurely exercise. Lexa's heart seemed to miss a beat as her eyes took in the attractiveness of him. His hair, not as immaculate as usual, was gleaming for all that, with those threads of silver, caught in the sunlight, standing out prominently from the darkness of the rest of his hair. He was dressed in pearl-grey slacks and a cotton jacket of lilac-blue fashioned in the draped line for a casual appearance. As he drew closer she saw the look of enquiry in his eyes, but apart from that his distinctive features were fixed, as usual, and unreadable.

Before he could question Lexa Evelyn Sharman was speaking, producing a winning smile as she said,

'Hello, Paul. Did you do all you wanted to do?'

'Yes,' he answered, then turned to Lexa. 'Where's Alacho?' He glanced significantly at his watch. 'Is she in the schoolroom?'

Lexa shook her head.

'She needs a doctor, Mr Mansell; she's not very well. I left her sleeping, and have been trying to ring the doctor. I'll try again now—or perhaps you'll do it?'

'She's not well?' A frown touched his brow. Lexa felt his anxiety and rejoiced at it. Evelyn Sharman's eyes were fixed upon his face, watching his expression intently. 'Have you any idea what can be wrong with her?'

'It's nothing serious,' she hastened to assure him, but added that she would prefer the doctor to be called in any case.

'It's probably something she's eaten,' drawled Evelyn, bored. 'I've been trying to reassure Miss Duke, but she's obviously one of those people who panic easily.'

Lexa gasped, her temper rising, but as before she was able to maintain her calm.

'I certainly don't panic easily, Mrs Sharman. I'm naturally concerned about the child in my charge, but I assure you I've had far too much experience with young children and their minor ailments to panic simply because Alacho's off colour.' She had forgotten the presence of her employer altogether, but his eyes, burning into her, brought hers upwards, to notice the most odd expression, the sort of expression that revealed anger, but not against her! Against Mrs Sharman, then? There was something about the present situation that affected Lexa profoundly, created a tenseness within her as if something of vital importance was about to take place.

'You say you've been trying to ring the doctor, Miss Duke,' said Paul anxiously. 'You couldn't get him?'

She shook her head.

'I think there's something wrong with the line—or there was when I was trying to get through. It might be all right now.'

'I'll have a try, and if I can't get through I'll go and see if I can get him. He might be out, though, in which case I'll have to leave a message.'

Lexa went to the nursery and to Alacho's bedroom. She had wakened and seemed to be her normal self, her colour had returned, her voice was lively as she said she was getting up.

Lexa sighed. She had had children at school who'd had to be taken to the rest room, and who had been as right as rain after a little sleep in the warmth and the quiet.

'Are you sure you're better?'

'I feel fine! It was my tummy—I think. It felt fuzzy—all moving and——'

'Never mind,' interrupted Lexa, too relieved to feel foolish at her anxiety. 'Come on, then, and I'll dress you.'

'I can do it myself. I nearly always do. It was something I ate,' Alacho added with a frown. 'I didn't much like the pudding and custard we had yesterday.'

'It wasn't pudding; it was apple tart.'

'Yes, that's right. It made me feel sick.'

'Why didn't you tell me?'

'Because it went away again and I wasn't sick. I'm glad I wasn't, because it's horrible with all that in your mouth and——'

'Alacho, for heaven's sake stop!'

The child only laughed at her nanny's revolted expression.

'It would seem,' came a suave voice from the door, 'that you've made a rapid recovery, Alacho.' Her father came slowly into the room, his eyes intently fixed on Lexa, an unfathomable expression beneath the hint of amusement which was also reflected in the slant at one corner of his mouth.

'Daddy! Were you worried about me? Did Lexa tell you I was in bed poorly?'

'She did, and yes, I was worried about you. That's why I'm here. But obviously both your nanny and I have worried unnecessarily.'

'Do I have to do lessons this afternoon—to make up for this morning?' Alacho was pulling her dainty silk and lace nightie over her head as she spoke. 'I will if you want, but I'd rather go swimming in the sea.' She stood there, naked, a slender little thing with bronzed body—bronzed but for a tiny white triangle where the scant covering had been. Her father stared for a long moment, as if seeing something he had never seen before, and Lexa wondered just how long it was since he had seen his daughter naked. Not since she was a small baby, she decided, a baby of about one year old.

He spoke at last, to say quietly,

'That's up to Miss Duke. If she says you must do your lessons then you do them.'

'How is she——?' Evelyn had come to the door and all three occupants of the room turned. 'She doesn't look ill to me!'

'I'm better! It was the apple tart and custard. It made me feel sick, but I'm better now. The sick didn't come!' ended Alacho triumphantly.

Evelyn stared at the naked child and to Lexa's amazement she saw that the girl was faintly embarrassed. Incredible! Had she never seen a naked child before? It was obvious that she had never had children of her own.

'I said it was something she'd eaten,' said Evelyn scoffingly as her eyes went to Lexa. 'Paul, don't you think she should be getting dressed?' Again that trace of embarrassment. Lexa wondered what kind of life the girl had lived, to be embarrassed by a sight such as this. It then dawned upon her that she, Lexa, was different. In her role of infant teacher she was always faced with the possibility of accidents, and in fact, every infant school made provisions in the form of a stock of underwear, both for girls and boys. Lexa could never hope to estimate the number of times she had changed her children. It was one task that was taken for granted in the same way that tying shoelaces or wiping noses was taken. Yes, she was different, and was soon admitting that she ought not to be criticising the other woman.

'I *am* getting dressed,' said Alacho unnecessarily as she slipped into a pair of frilly panties. 'I'm going swimming after lunch, though, aren't I, Lexa?'

'Yes, I think we'll skip the lessons for today.'

'Goody!' Alacho looked at her father, and after a pause said persuasively, 'Will you come swimming with us, Daddy? You did once and you said it was very nice. Do you remember?'

'Yes, I remember.'

'So will you come again today?'

'Perhaps I will,' he said after a small pause during which he read the plea in Lexa's eyes. 'Yes, it will be pleasant in the sea today.'

Lexa's glance shifted to Mrs Sharman's face. It was set and pale, and her eyes were narrowed beneath a frowning brow. Obviously the girl was not pleased by Paul's decision.

When Lexa met Jeremy that evening he asked again about a possible visit to Bangkok.

'I don't know,' she returned doubtfully. 'I haven't had an opportunity of asking Mr Mansell about it yet.'

'Not had an opportunity?' with a slight lift of his brows. 'You see him every day. And for most of this afternoon you were on the beach with him.'

'Alacho was there, and Mrs Sharman, his friend whom I mentioned.'

'Yes, I noticed his friend was there too. Good-looking piece but hard, I should say.'

'I didn't see you——' Lexa turned to him, puzzled. 'You didn't come close enough to see her properly.'

'Oh, yes, I did. I was strolling along the beach when you and your boss were swimming. You didn't see me.'

They had reached a small path leading off from the beach and into the thick, tropical vegetation that occupied the backshore, and by common consent they both turned on to it. They had found a pretty spot by a tiny waterfall where a myriad wild flowers grew, mainly orchids. It was an idyllic place by day, when the mid-afternoon sun wove a tapestry of incandescent colour—dazzling scarlet and emerald, magenta and every shade of gold. At night it was equally fascinating to Lexa, with the pungent smell of dampness replacing the heady scent of flowers, the multitude of mauves and lilacs, and the mysterious duns and greys replacing the brighter, more tangible colours which were the art-work of the sun. She loved to feel the spray from the cascade on her face and hair, the softness of moss beneath her feet, loved to have a moth touch her cheek, to hear the night-insects trilling in the trees. With the going of the sun the air became cool and fresh, and when there was a moon everywhere was tinted with silver. It was a romantic spot, the place where a girl ought to be with the man of her dreams.

And much as she liked Jeremy, Lexa had no false ideas that he was the man of her dreams.

'Shall we sit down?' He had brought a waterproof, which he spread on a rock-ledge, and she sat down, while Jeremy stood for a moment in the darkness, looking at her.

'What is it?' she asked as the silence stretched. She was uneasy, her nerves tensed. 'Aren't you going to sit down?'

'In a minute.' He gave her a tender smile. 'Lexa....'

'Yes?'

'You know how it is with me, don't you?'

Lexa's heart jumped. She feigned bewilderment as she said,

'With you, Jeremy?'

'Don't prevaricate. I love you, Lexa, and you know it. A woman always does.' His voice was low and anxious. She knew that to him this was a vital moment in his life and she was hating herself for encouraging him in the way she had, avidly seeking his company, enjoying their strolls on the beach, their visits to the café. And especially she had delighted in these moments here, away from the unaccustomed anxieties that had entered her life since she took the post of nanny to Alacho. This spot was a haven of peace to which no one else had, as yet, come to intrude on the privacy which she and Jeremy enjoyed. Here, beneath a vibrant starlit tropical sky, she had always been able to sink into a sublime, delicious lassitude, chatting with her companion. But now her voice was frozen to silence as remorse and self-blame shot through her. It wasn't as if she hadn't known. No, there was no excuse behind which she could hide her guilt. Jeremy had openly admitted from the first that he 'liked' her, and she knew what that really meant. As he had just said, a woman knows when a man loves her.

She sighed, her thoughts switching to that time when she had asked herself what she wanted, when she wished fervently that she knew what her own dreams and desires were. Her association with the stolid Joe was one she had been able to understand and control from the first; both he and she knew that nothing serious would come of it. With Jeremy it had been different in some way; they had been closer, more intimate in their conversation. As she had realised from the first, Jeremy had been going too fast for her.

He spoke, softly, anxiously, breaking into thoughts that had brought shadows to her eyes.

'Lexa dear. . . . You do care, if only a little? I couldn't bear it if you were to tell me you don't care at all.'

'I don't know what to—to say. I feel—terrible about this. . . .' She stopped, slowly, another sigh escaping her.

Everything had lost its brightness; even the stars seemed dimmer than usual. 'Jeremy, I did say, if you remember, that people had to get to know one another.'

Even as she spoke her mind was recalling her very early conviction that she would fall in love at first sight. Well, it would seem that she was not now of the same opinion. A couple ought to get to know one another. Marriage was too precarious a step to take without at least making an attempt beforehand to ensure its success. And running blindly into it could not possibly make for success—not unless by some miracle those concerned were exceptionally lucky.

'You don't love me, then?' Jeremy's voice was blank, as devoid of expression as his face. 'I suppose I should have known it.'

'I did tell you that the right man hadn't come along,' she reminded him.

'I know, but your attitude lately——' He turned from her broodingly. 'It gave me hope because you seemed to enjoy being with me.'

'I have enjoyed being with you, Jeremy. And I'd still enjoy it, but I suppose you won't want to see me any more.'

'Would you miss these strolls we have, and the few minutes we sit here, in this spot we've found?'

'Of course I'd miss it all—everything we've done together.'

'And yet you could end it, here and now?' His tone had changed, a bitterness entering into it. 'I wish I'd never come here this time. I did toy with the idea of going on a trip to Egypt with a couple of friends but decided against it because of Mum and Dad, who look forward to seeing me once a year.' He looked at her unhappily. 'If I hadn't come I'd never have met you.'

'I'm sorry.' How inadequate! He was genuinely upset and Lexa knew for sure that he would not get over it as quickly as she would have liked him to. 'We've not had a chance, not really,' she added in a gentle tone. 'These meetings, short because of my job; the knowledge that you're only here for a month——'

'What has that to do with it?'

'Well ... one is conscious of a certain urgency....' She tailed off, not in any way sure what she wanted to say.

'If there was urgency then it was only on your side. I was ready to continue our—friendship by correspondence if need be.' His tone was persuasive and as he sat down beside her he took both her hands in his. 'Let's do just that, Lexa—please, dear, say we can write to one another?'

'What's the use, Jeremy? I don't care enough. Besides, there's Alacho. I'd never leave her while she needs me the way she does at present.'

He cast her a frowning, sideways glance.

'You wouldn't sacrifice your own life, surely?'

She shook her head uncertainly.

'If I fell madly in love I suppose I should have to make a decision. But as things are—well, Alacho's my first consideration.'

'This woman who's here,' he said, still frowning, 'is there anything between them?'

Lexa stiffened at the mention of Mrs Sharman.

'I don't know. I shouldn't think there's any possibility of marriage, if that's what she's hoping for.'

'Why?' The question was brief and sharp.

'Because of the way he always thinks of his dead wife.' Was Jeremy hoping that Paul would marry, and provide a mother for his child, thereby releasing Lexa from any obligation she felt for the child?

'Always? How do you know that?' His hands released hers and she sensed a coolness creeping into the atmosphere.

'It doesn't matter,' she answered, hoping to dismiss the subject. 'What time is it, Jeremy? I must be going in.'

'It's early—only a quarter to ten.'

'Late enough.' She stood up and moved away, thinking sadly that this would probably be the last time she would come to this enchanted spot, for she could never come by herself.

'Your voice was strange when you spoke of your boss just now.' Jeremy rose to his feet, coming up close beside her and staring down into her face, an odd expression in his eyes. 'Why are you so reticent when his name's mentioned? Why do you always change the subject?'

She answered with a touch of impatience.

'I don't want to discuss Mr Mansell, that's all.'

'Strange ... very strange....' He spoke softly, to himself, his eyes wide, and fixed as if he were deep in recollection. 'I remember on that very first occasion when I mentioned him—a trifle disparagingly, I admit—you blew me up and told me to mind my own business, or something of the sort. Even then I wondered....' Again he was musing to himself, lost in thought, although his glance had flickered over Lexa's face as if he wanted to note her reaction. 'You were so ready to defend him, weren't you? And since—whenever his name crops up, you instantly change the subject.'

Lexa frowned at him.

'What are you trying to say?' she asked bewilderedly.

'I've been struck by a sudden idea,' he answered cryptically. 'And I'm damned sure it's got some foundation.'

'I can't think what you mean,' she complained. 'What is this sudden idea as you term it?'

'Think about what I've said,' he recommended, a grim edge to his voice. 'Think about it and examine your own feelings ... where your boss is concerned!' He turned from her, swinging away along the shore, leaving her standing there, her thoughts tangling themselves into knots of confusion so that for a few moments nothing clear emerged. And then she drew a breath, a long incredulous breath as she stood there, endeavouring to detach herself from the devastating knowledge that was striving to break through into her consciousness.

It was impossible! This was not her destiny—to love a man as unattainable as the stars! She was not such a fool! She knew—anyone in her right mind would know— that Paul Mansell was still married to the mother of his child. He would never ever be free, simply because the prison he was in was of his own making, and the walls around it were impregnable.

For how long she stood there Lexa did not know. It could have been minutes, or hours. Time had no meaning; the only thing that did have meaning was that she had fallen wildly, irrevocably, in love with a man whom she could never hope to have as her husband.

CHAPTER EIGHT

LEXA was alone in the light, airy schoolroom when Paul entered. Alacho was in the garden, playing with Pango and one of the gardeners, and Lexa had considered it a good opportunity for doing a little clearing up, both in the room itself and in the drawers of her desk. She had one drawer pulled out and its contents scattered about untidily on the desk when she glanced up on hearing the door open.

'Ah, here you are, Miss Duke. Come to my study, please. I have something to say to you.'

She looked at him enquiringly, then averted her head. She had not wanted to see him so soon after the discovery she had made last evening. This morning she had avoided him quite easily, as she and Alacho always breakfasted together nowadays. And immediately after breakfast they had come to the schoolroom. Lunch was another meal they took together and then their practice was to go out, either on to the seashore or into the garden. Today, though, Alacho had gone off on seeing the gardener playing with the dog, and Lexa, instead of following, had taken one look around and decided to have half an hour or so doing something more productive than playing outside, especially as her presence was not necessary anyway.

'You want me—me to come now, Mr Mansell?' she said, and he nodded abruptly, saying yes, he wanted her at once.

She followed him into the hall and into a high arched passageway from which he entered his study.

'Sit down,' he flicked a hand towards a chair. 'I won't waste time,' he commented a few seconds later. 'I understand you and Mrs Bardsley's son are—friendly? Perhaps I should say, more than friendly?'

She coloured, deeply embarrassed by his piercing scrutiny.

'Not *more* than friendly,' she said.

'Mrs Sharman seems to think that you are. You meet him every evening after Alacho's in bed.'

Lexa's eyes blazed.

'How the—— How does she know what my movements are?'

Paul was by the window, standing erect, so tall and overpowering. She wished she had not sat down, for she felt small, inferior. Yet on the other hand, she was in a temper, trying to visualise how Mrs Sharman had discovered what she did in the evenings.

'She takes a stroll sometimes. She tells me that you and he——' A hand was lifted imperiously to stop the interruption Lexa was about to make. 'It's your own affair, Miss Duke, but I must know if there's any possibility of your leaving me in the near future?'

She began to shake her head, furious that Mrs Sharman should have carried that information to Paul.

'I shan't be leaving you, Mr Mansell....' Her voice trailed and she glanced down, to her hands, clasped in her lap. Last night, as she lay wakeful through the long weary hours, she had reached the conclusion that she must leave here, get away from Paul altogether—go home and try to forget she had been so foolish as to fall in love with him. But inevitably her own problem had been blotted out by the picture of Alacho, who needed her, who would need her until she had the love of her father. How long would that be? Lexa had asked herself.

She had left Paul and Alacho together that afternoon, swimming in the warm sea. Evelyn Sharman, preferring to remain on the beach, had sat there with a book, a tight expression on her face. Paul's manner with his child was certainly undergoing a change, slowly but very definitely. Lexa had shown him her work every day, trying to hold his interest, and she was winning. Yes, she was winning, and it was a warm, satisfied feeling which she experienced on those occasions when he spent some time with his daughter. His voice was now always gentle when he spoke to her and Lexa had seen his eyes become filled with a sort of wonderment when he looked into the beautiful little face, and Lexa would watch intently, aware that he was seeing his daughter at last, recognising her charming little ways, her beauty and, more important, he was accepting that she needed his love.

'You don't seem too sure?' Paul's voice carried a strange inflection, and for no reason that she could explain Lexa's mind raced back to an instant in time when she had felt that something of vital importance was about to happen. The idea had been forgotten, but now it was with her again, stronger than ever because of the quality of her employer's voice and the steady, direct way he was looking into her eyes, searching, probing. . . .

'I am sure, Mr Mansell. There's nothing serious between Jeremy and me.'

'A flirtation, then?' His voice was faintly contemptuous but his eyes still retained that steadfast look.

She reddened and for a moment could find no words to answer him. Was it a flirtation on her part? She supposed it was, and bit her lip, ashamed that she had allowed Jeremy to kiss her.

'It was a—friendship,' she managed at last, 'which has now ended.'

'Ended ... altogether?' he asked slowly, and she looked swiftly at him, for he had drawn a breath which she could only interpret as relief.

'Yes, altogether,' she answered, thinking that it was most unlikely she would ever see Jeremy again. Certainly they would never meet as they had been doing. She thought of the way he had hit upon the truth even before she herself had recognised it. He must be feeling terribly bitter, she thought, blaming herself once again for allowing the affair to go as far as it had. 'You've been anxious? You thought you might be having to look for another nanny?' She wasn't sure why she said this— unless it was to end the silence, which was stretching uncomfortably because Paul, who had taken possession of a chair opposite to her, was staring in front of him, giving her the impression that he had almost forgotten she was there at all.

He looked at her as she spoke, and shook his head.

'I felt that boarding-school was the only way. I'd no intention, at that time, of trying even yet again to find a nanny for her.'

'At that time?' repeated Lexa, her eyes flying to his, a question in their depths.

'Yes, at that time——'

'But not now?' she just had to say, a lovely wa[...] spreading over her. 'Now, Mr Mansell, you love [...] too much to send her away.' It was a statement, b[...] the question was still in her eyes. He nodded and said gently,

'I have a lot to thank you for, Miss Duke. You made

in Pattaya. When my father died I came into his proper-
ties in Bangkok, and also the half share of the hotels in
Pattaya. Mr Gifford and I got along fine; there was never
one disagreement as to how the hotels would be run. But
he died while I was in England a few months ago and
his daughter inherited.'

He stopped because Lexa was nodding, quite mechanically, because she was recalling how, when she had
asked him once about the hotels he owned, his face had
hardened as if something was angering him. It was plain
to her now that he had been thinking of Mrs Sharman,
and that she was now part owner of the hotels in Pattaya.
'She began interfering immediately,' Paul continued. 'She
demands that the staff be drastically reduced; she wants
the standard lowering, with a cheap tariff so that only
package tour groups will be catered for. She's the most
avaricious, mercenary woman I've ever known, and all
she wants is more and more money from the hotels. I've
tried repeatedly to conduct our business together har-
moniously, but it's futile to make any effort at all.' Again
he paused and Lexa waited, quite unable to see where
she came into it, but she was soon to know. 'Mr Gifford
knew his daughter well, apparently, for he made a will
which gave her the shares in the hotels, but, should I
marry, she was to sell out to me, totally.'

Lexa blinked.

'That was a strange thing for a father to do,' she
frowned.

Paul hesitated as if reluctant to comment on that, but
eventually he gave a resigned shrug of his shoulders and
said that Mrs Sharman had confided to her father that
she would like to marry his partner.

'Whenever I was over here, even though I was married, she acted shamelessly——' He stopped, frowned,

then said brusquely, 'I think you'll know what I mean without my going into details?'

'Yes, I understand,' she said. The woman had flirted with him, she supposed, or tried to.

'Well, Mr Gifford must have realised that, if I did happen to marry someone else, she would make life pretty unpleasant for me, so he put that clause in his will in order to safeguard me.'

'It was thoughtful of him.'

'As I've said, he and I got along fine, and so did he and my father. There was no reason why his daughter could not have adopted the same reasonable attitude, but for some reason she's chosen to be awkward.'

For some reason.... Because he had not offered to marry her, decided Lexa, and then, as the thought occurred to her, she asked him why, if he disliked Mrs Sharman so much, he had her here now as his guest.

'It was at her suggestion,' he explained. 'She said we might be able to resolve our many differences if we talked in some atmosphere away from the hotels, away from Bangkok. I rather think,' he added, looking at her, 'that she was curious to see you. She'd asked me about Alacho's new nanny and I described you to her——' He cut the rest, but he had said enough to make Lexa blush, as it was obvious that the description had not pleased Mrs Sharman. Paul's next words proved her conclusion to be correct. 'She had expected me to get someone much older.' He smiled one of his rare smiles as he added, 'Alacho needed a mature spinster, she told me.'

Lexa's blush deepened and for a moment he stared at her, his eyes intently taking in the delicate contours of her face, the grave expression, the tremulous movement of her lips.

'Apparently her plan to resolve your differences didn't

come to anything?' murmured Lexa presently.

'Her idea of a solution was for us to marry,' he commented, and Lexa's eyes flew to his.

'*She* didn't suggest marriage, surely?'

'And very calm she was about it too,' mused Paul, far away all at once. 'For her it would have been mainly a business deal. She'd have come into everything if I died, for I'm sure she would have found a way of robbing my child.' He looked at Lexa and added, 'My love for Alacho is one reason for my wanting to marry. I don't wish to have her robbed——'

'Oh, don't say such things!' cried Lexa. 'You're not going to die!'

He regarded her with an odd expression, but all he said was,

'None of us knows, so we can't say. All we can do is to try and make things easier for those who are left, which is exactly what Mr Gifford did for me,' he ended significantly, his eyes never leaving Lexa's face.

'I—I——' She floundered, her eyes misty all at once. 'It wouldn't work——'

'So you've said already. Sleep on it,' he advised, 'and give me your answer tomorrow.'

Sleep on it. . . .

That was what Miss Saunders had recommended, and the result was that Lexa had found herself swayed from her resolve to turn down the post offered by the man who was now offering her marriage.

How would Mrs Sharman take it if she did agree to marry Paul? She would be furious, inevitably wishing she had not gone so far, had refrained from driving Paul in the way she had been doing. Well, if he did marry there was nothing for her but to sell out because that was stated quite clearly in her father's will.

*

Sleep.... How easy to tell anyone to sleep! Lexa, having tossed and turned for most of the night, rose at five o'clock, unable to lie there any longer. She went to the kitchen and made a pot of tea, having to pass Mrs Sharman's bedroom door as she moved silently on the thick carpet covering the landing.

She believed she had been unheard and was naturally startled when, having switched on the kettle, she turned around to find herself face to face with the woman she had disliked from the moment she set eyes upon her.

'Oh ... you made me—me jump!'

'Did I? I'm sorry.' Mrs Sharman was in a glamorous wrap of vivid blue velvet trimmed with satin. Her hair had been combed and automatically Lexa pushed a hand through her own, all too conscious of her dishevelled appearance.

'Do you want something?' she enquired, wondering why her heart was beating so quickly.

'You're making tea? Obviously you couldn't sleep?'

'It was one of those nights.' Lexa turned away, to find the teapot and the tea-bags which she knew were kept in a small earthenware pot on a shelf by the sink.

'Something on your mind?' Soft the tone but insolent, and Lexa swung around, eyes glinting.

'I don't think I understand you, Mrs Sharman. Why are you here?'

'I heard you pass my door—at least, I knew someone was passing and I got out of bed to investigate. I saw you and thought I'd come and see what you were up to.'

'Up to?' Sparks of fire were ignited from the glints already in Lexa's eyes. 'Would you mind explaining?'

The woman moved, with the grace of a queen, and took possession of a chair, crossing her legs as she sat down. The wrap came open to reveal a diaphanous nightdress underneath. Lexa glanced away and busied herself with the teapot, dropping a couple of tea-bags into it.

'Are you happy here, Miss Duke?' came the unexpected question and, before Lexa had time to answer, 'I wonder how you would react to an offer I'm willing to make.' The words came purringly and Lexa shivered. She recalled Miss Saunders once describing a particularly obnoxious mother as unwholesome. There was something decidedly unwholesome about the woman sitting there, outwardly immaculate ... yes, outwardly....

'Offer?' Lexa was curious, her gaze interrogating. 'You have an offer to make to me?'

'I've just said so,' replied Mrs Sharman arrogantly. 'How would you like to pocket a couple of thousand pounds?'

Lexa's eyes narrowed with perception. Nevertheless she did ask what the offer entailed.

'You're interested, then?' Mrs Sharman asked, her eyes alive for the first time. 'It's a lot of money——'

'Oh, I wouldn't say that,' interrupted Lexa, unable to resist playing a game with the detestable creature. 'These days it's not much at all—not even six months' salary.'

'It isn't?' with a frown of disbelief. 'You rate yourself high, Miss Duke.'

Lexa shrugged, noticed the kettle was boiling and turned her back on the woman.

'Your offer,' she said casually, 'what is it?'

'I'm willing to pay you two thousand pounds to leave here,' Evelyn Sharman replied slowly, her narrowed gaze fixed on Lexa's back.

'Two thousand, to give up a job like this!' With a glance of contempt Lexa turned, and it was in that moment that all her doubts melted, that she knew where her destiny lay. She would do anything—*anything*, to rescue Paul from the vicious unscrupulousness of this woman. 'What sort of a fool do you take me for? And why is it so important to you that I leave here?' She knew, of course, but she was interested to know what sort of a reply she would get.

The other woman's mouth twisted; her eyes were dark with hate.

'Never mind. I have my reasons! I'll make it three thousand,' she spat out. 'You'd be crazy to refuse! You could go straight back and get a job, in your profession, and you'd have the three thousand as clear profit.'

Lexa poured the water into the teapot and put down the kettle. It was obvious that Evelyn Sharman considered her to be a danger to her own ambitions, but as yet it had not dawned on her that she had already gone too far with Paul, had tried his patience beyond its limits. Lexa could not help wondering what she would say were she to tell her that Paul had proposed marriage to her, and that she had decided to accept his proposal. However, all she said was,

'There's nothing you could offer that would tempt me,' and on that she went out, leaving the woman sitting there, her face twisted into a line so ugly that it was hardly recognisable.

They were married in Bangkok, at the Church of Christ in Phetchaburi Road. Paul brought two friends and that was all. They were English, Miles and Annabel Bowers, who had a Thai silk shop in Suriwong Road and lived in a flat above it. For Lexa the whole ceremony was unreal; she could not assimilate the fact that she was being married at all, much less to Paul Mansell, a man she had once hated ... a man who would probably never love her, and even if he did, his love could never be as strong as the love he had had for Alacho's mother.

What had she done? The question had come to her several times since she told Paul that she would marry him, but now, in the church, after having taken the vows, she was sickeningly conscious of a heavy weight rising up, through her body, over her heart, to settle somewhere between throat and chest.

'Are you all right?' asked Paul, and his voice was anxious, she thought.

'Yes—fine,' she answered, rallying as best she could. Why was she so afraid? She had known what she was doing, had accepted what was offered without consciously expecting anything else. It was a business arrangement—not, granted, quite so cold-blooded an arrangement as it would have been had Paul married Mrs Sharman, but a business contract just the same. She would be a wife in name only, so she could not expect children. She would have her husband's confidence in the running of the home and the bringing up of his child, but she would not have his love. How could she hide her own love indefinitely? This was what she feared. Yes, it was suddenly brought home to her that the most difficult part of her marriage would be to control any impulse to reveal her love.

The meal was a happy one, though, taken in the Normandie Grill where they were waited on as if they had been royalty. Annabel was a delightful woman whose spontaneous smile had won Lexa over immediately she had been introduced to her the day before the wedding, when she and Paul had come to the hotel, leaving Alacho in the capable care of Maria. How delighted the child had been! The recollection brought a smile to Lexa's face and her husband, sitting opposite to her, sent her a questioning glance.

'I was thinking about Alacho,' she said. 'She was so happy.'

'She's a dear child.' Annabel went on to say that she had seen her only a few times, but had found her enchanting. 'She ought to be happy, having a mummy now as well as a daddy.'

Lexa glanced at Paul, hesitantly. He was smiling and she could not help but wonder if the smile was forced. However, both Miles and his wife seemed determined to make Lexa happy, and she fell to musing on just how much they knew. From what Lexa had gathered the previous evening when she and Paul had dined with them, it would seem that although they were friends of his they were certainly not close friends. He had no close friends; he had admitted as much to Lexa. He kept himself to himself and it had surprised Lexa that he had anyone at all to call upon to assist with the wedding.

'You must come into the shop,' Miles said when it was time for them to leave. 'Choose some lengths of silk, and have them from us—as a wedding present.'

'Thank you very much. I'll be in the next time I come to Bangkok.'

They went soon afterwards and Lexa was left alone with her husband. Never had she felt so awkward, so lost for words, so eager to escape. They had used the suite last night and were using it again tonight, and she would have done anything to be able to go to her room, to relax in the cool bed . . . and think. Yet was it wise to think too much about what she had done? She was still rather dazed, unable to grasp the fact that she was a wife. It dawned on her that she was now a stepmother, a circumstance that left her a little awed, since being a mother seemed to entail so much more than being a mere nanny. Greater demands would be made upon her; much more would be expected of her, and decisions would inevitably have to be made as the years went by.

'You're very quiet, Lexa.' Paul's voice brought her out of her reverie; she coloured, not yet used to his calling her Lexa.

'I was thinking,' she answered, and he naturally asked what she was thinking about. 'Alacho,' she replied. 'I'm a stepmother. It's a little frightening,' she added, and saw him lift his brows a fraction.

'Frightening? Why?'

'There'll be more responsibility.'

'That won't trouble you.' He looked at her kindly. 'Don't worry, Lexa, you'll make a success of this, I know you will.'

Such confidence brought added colour to her lovely face.

'It's the idea of marriage without—without love that makes me afraid,' she said, a tremor in her voice.

'You were talking about Alacho,' he reminded her, 'not us.'

She nodded, but said after a pause,

'It's all mixed up, Paul. I expect I shall sort everything out in my mind eventually.' And fall into a routine, she thought ... a routine not much different from that existing at present. An unloved wife. ... Her lip quivered but she managed to hold back the moisture that would have come to her eyes. 'It's been so hurried, and I'm still confused.' She had no idea just how young and helpless she looked, how vulnerable, like a child who was floundering, seeking for security and love.

Paul's voice was gentle when he said,

'I think we'll stay here, in Bangkok, for a few days. It will give us the chance to get to know one another.'

Her eyes lit up.

'That'll be lovely, Paul. Thank you for being so thoughtful and—and kind.' She was full up but that terrible weight had lifted and the future was not quite so vague and frightening as it had been a short while ago. If Paul was going to be as kind as this then life would be good! She would ask no more, not yet. One day ... in the distant future when the pain within him had been eased for ever he might turn to her, and love her a little, just a little. She would be satisfied with that, she told herself confidently.

But how little she knew....

CHAPTER NINE

THEIR 'honeymoon' began that same evening when they dined on the riverside terrace of the Royal Palm Hotel, in an elegant candlelit atmosphere, dined on choicest seafood washed down with vintage wines. At half-past nine a group of Thai dancers took the floor against a background of gongs and cymbals, their elaborately-jewelled, brocaded costumes and masks and high pointed helmets copied from patterns hundreds of years old.

'This is a classical Thai dance,' Paul told Lexa, then went on to explain that, in its purest form, it was called *Khon*. 'The version being performed,' he added, 'is the Thai version of the very famous Indian epic, the Ramayana, and the Thais call it the Ramakien.'

Fascinated, Lexa watched the girls—in bare feet—gliding rhythmically, arms curving, snake-like, sensuous. Their hands were open to represent lotus cups, their fingers ornamented with gleaming metal that gave Lexa the impression of an animal's claws.

'It's really a masked pantomime, isn't it?' she said, looking at Paul across the dinner table.

He nodded.

'Yes, it is, and you'll see that a female takes the hero's part, just as in a pantomime in England. Boys play the parts of the Monkey King, though, and his demons.'

'Is the hero someone from history?' asked Lexa interestedly.

'Of course: Rama, the first legendary King of Siam.

He was so revered that every king since his time is given the honorary title of King Rama.'

'It's ... wonderful. ...' Lexa was in a dream, for all this spelt magic, this setting of moonlit river and beautiful tropical landscaped gardens, with the performers in their glittering gold, swaying to the music, playing out the epic whose sequel must be death to the king's enemy.

The end came, with the dancers leaving the stage to a tremendous spate of clapping and spontaneous applause.

'Enjoy it?' Paul seemed faintly amused by Lexa's glowing face. 'It's a popular dance which is performed here every night.'

'It was wonderful! It might be ordinary to you,' she added, noticing his expression, 'but to me it's new—and I could see it again and again.'

'It isn't ordinary even to me,' he denied. 'There's so much talent, so much grace of movement, that one never tires of that kind of dancing.' His voice was quiet, timbred with that brogue he had inherited from his mother. Lexa saw that his gaze was concentrated on her, was aware too of a trace of annoyance in their steely depths and was for no reason at all reminded of another occasion when he had regarded her with this kind of concentration. She had gained the impression that he was angry with himself for seeing things he would rather not have seen. Was he beginning to find some attraction in her? Had he seen something attractive on that other occasion? It would be understandable that, determined to keep the memory of his dead wife alive, he would hate the idea of finding some other woman attractive.

The dessert course was brought—a delicious coconut concoction served in the shell—and then to her surprise and pleasure he asked her to dance.

She stood up, every nerve quivering at the idea of being held in his arms, of feeling his body close to hers. His face, unsmiling, was far above hers and her head came only to his shoulder. Paul danced with perfect yet casual precision, with Lexa following with similar grace and ease of movement, her feet seeming to touch nothing but a cushion of air. It was intoxicating, with the music and the perfume of flowers, palms swaying against the night sky, forming mystic silhouettes pierced by points of light, glittering like diamonds. Stars, millions of them in the clear, purple-dark heavens.... An ache rose in Lexa's throat, an ache for what might have been if only Paul had been in love with her. The yearning passed, however, and she was again thrilling to what was hers, thrusting away from her conscious thoughts what was beyond her reach.

'You dance excellently.' Paul's voice carried a hint of enthusiasm which convinced her at once that he had once enjoyed dancing. He held her from him as he spoke; her face was flushed and beautiful, her lips quivering and parted, her eyes glowing, happy—and hiding, she hoped, what was in her heart. She saw his own eyes widen and knew without any doubt that he did see something attractive about her. But as before that frown appeared, faint it was true, but there all the same, and his lids came down to veil his expression.

Back at their table, they were given coffee and liqueurs, with a small bowl of sweetmeats which Paul ignored but which proved far too tempting for Lexa to resist.

'Are you tired?' he asked when they had finished, and after they had had another dance together. 'It's very late,' he added before she could reply, 'so you must be.'

She could have stayed longer, and danced again and again, but she could see that her husband was ready to go back to the hotel, so she said with a smile,

'Yes, Paul, it is late, and I do feel rather tired.'

They took a taxi, sitting in silence, and inevitably she became conscious that this was her wedding day. Pictures formed even though she did not want them, mental visions of what—in the days of her dreams—she had expected her honeymoon to be like. Tender glances and caresses, loving words whispered, cheek to cheek, hands clasped, and, at this time of the night, hearts beating overrate with the thrill of expectancy, with heaven only a breath away.

Once in their suite Paul asked if she wanted anything to drink and when she declined a silence fell between them, awkward and prolonged. What was he thinking? It seemed that he must be dwelling on that other wedding day, when love was there, when, at this hour, he would probably have his bride in his arms, her body yielding to his mastery.

God, what have I done! The conviction that she had made a terrible mistake was so overpowering that she could have cried out, telling him that she already regretted her decision and that he must free her! Instead, she managed to control even her voice as she said, breaking the silence at last,

'I'm going to bed, Paul. Goodnight—and thank you for a lovely evening.'

He looked at her, his face taut, his eyes darkly brooding.

'Goodnight, Lexa. Sleep well.'

The following morning they had breakfast in the suite, then cruised along the Chao Phya River on the luxury *Oriental Queen*, starting at the early hour of eight o'clock for the whole-day trip to the ancient ruins of Ayudhya, one-time capital of Siam. The sun was shining, the river smooth, its muddy waters a hive of activity, with its boats of all sizes and shapes. A long row of sampans was being towed by a motor-boat, women were doing their laundry from the bank, chatting together and smiling. Lexa, fascinated by the complex riverine activity, realised that the river and the numerous *klongs* branching off it was even in these times still the scene of an ancient Thai way of life.

'It's all so new, and strange,' she murmured, glancing at Paul to see if he was taking as much interest in all the activity as she. He smiled at her, bringing a swift glow to her eyes. 'Just look at the gleaming buildings, Paul, the lovely temples and the graceful Thai houses.' They were built on stilts and shaded with palms. He said nothing and she sat back in her seat and continued to watch the passing procession of river life.

They had lunch on board at the Summer Palace of Bang-Pa-in, then boarded a coach for the tour of the ancient ruins of Ayudhya.

'It's so overgrown,' said Lexa sadly as she and Paul strolled around on their own, gazing up at the ruins of some of the three hundred and twenty-seven temples which had been built to the glory of Buddha and later destroyed by the Burmese, never to rise again.

'The weeds are even growing up the sides of the temples.'

'And birds nesting and roosting in the *prangs*.' Even as he spoke two massive black birds sailed over their heads to come to rest on one of the tall pinnacles.

It was five o'clock in the afternoon by the time they got back to the hotel, Lexa tired but happy, Paul very quiet and thoughtful, as he had been for most of the day. Lexa found herself saying, as they sat in the Garden

Lounge eating a light snack and drinking coffee,

'Paul—are you bored?'

The question seemed to startle him and his expression became apologetic.

'Not by any means, Lexa, though I know I've been quiet all day.' He looked at her, his face serene, the scar pale—still very noticeable but by no means as ugly as it sometimes was. 'You'll get used to me,' he assured her, faintly smiling. 'I've already told you that I'm not a communicative man.'

'But you were different once,' she murmured almost to herself, and he knew what she meant.

He nodded in agreement. Once or twice his late wife had been mentioned—briefly—and he had spoken of her without emotion—at least, without any visible sign of emotion.

'Yes,' he admitted, 'I was different once.'

'Time,' she said, 'is said to help us forget.' Her big eyes were shadowed, but a mistiness came through, as she looked at him, framed as she was in a cluster of hibiscus bushes growing in a bed behind her.

'Yes, that's true, Lexa. Already it's all beginning to hurt less.'

'But it still hurts?' She had no idea why she should want to talk of the tragedy. Was it something morbid within her? she wondered.

'Yes, it still hurts——' He looked straight at her, his eyes narrowed. 'And it always will, Lexa.'

She felt her heart freeze within her, for the warning had come through quite plainly: she must never hope to win his love. Had he some idea, then, of her own feelings for him? She frowned inwardly and resolved to be less friendly, to adopt the same cool affability with him as he was adopting with her.

The following day they visited the Grand Palace, which was in effect a cluster of magnificent Thai-style buildings enclosed within white castellated walls, with an imposing gateway where once elephants in jewelled trappings carried reigning monarchs to the inner palaces.

'The Temple of the Emerald Buddha's over in that corner.' Paul took Lexa's arm unexpectedly and led her over to where the temple—Wat Phra Keo—lay, the most impressive building in the entire compound. 'It's the private chapel of the King and Queen,' he added, and although Lexa knew this, having read it several times, she said nothing, afraid that he would not trouble to explain anything to her again. It was rather like being poised on a knife edge, she thought, afraid of offending him, desperately wanting him to talk to her. Conscious of the warmth of his hand beneath her elbow, she felt she scarcely dared turn, or take a false step that would make him withdraw his hand.

No cameras were allowed in the Temple of the Emerald Buddha, which was made of pure translucent jasper, not emerald. It sat under a canopy on a high pedestal elaborately embellished with gold leaf, and from somewhere unseen a subtle light was thrown on to the sacred image. Awed by the magnificence of the hauntingly beautiful figure, Lexa stood spellbound, recalling that this image was discovered when lightning had cracked open a pagoda and it was found, a stucco Buddha covered with gold leaf which later flaked off to reveal the green jasper underneath.

The rest of the Temple was in semi-darkness, and Lexa noticed several young women on their knees, lighting incense sticks and bowing their heads towards the marble floor in front of the shimmering green figure.

'What are those?' she was enquiring of her husband a

few minutes later as she saw other girls sinking to their knees and laying down some kind of offering.

'Sacred lotus buds,' he answered in a whisper. 'You'll have noticed that lotus flowers grow prolifically here, in the lakes and ponds.'

'Yes,' she murmured. 'I've seen them in flooded fields, too, when we were on the river yesterday.'

'The lotus is held to be sacred in Thailand, and even has its own special festival later in the year.'

He had withdrawn his hand but stood close, his body almost touching hers. She drew a shuddering breath, wishing she had the right to reach down and slip her hand into his.

Paul stirred, restlessly, and she felt sure a sigh had escaped him.

'Do you want to go?' she asked, and he nodded at once.

'I think so,' he answered, but stood there long enough to tell her that the Emerald Buddha was so greatly esteemed that no lesser a personage than the King himself could change its robes, which was performed in a solemn ceremony three times a year, for the rainy, hot and cool seasons.

'The robes are of pure gold, as you can see,' he went on, 'and they're studded with precious stones.'

'All that wealth—and just for one Buddha!'

'And there are thousands of Buddhas in Thailand.'

'The Golden Buddha—can we see that?'

'If you like.' His voice revealed nothing, but she knew instinctively that he was bored. However, they went to Wat Tramit, the Monastery of the Golden Buddha.

'Five and a half tons of solid gold,' Paul was saying as they stood and looked at the glittering image, worth over twenty million pounds. 'It was covered with plaster to protect it from the plundering Burmese invaders and was not discovered to be solid gold until about twenty-five years ago when, owing to a slight mishap, the plaster cracked.'

Her eyes widened.

'Can you imagine the surprise when they discovered what was beneath the plaster!'

'It must have been exciting, I admit.'

'How old will it be?' Lexa asked curiously.

'About seven hundred years,' he said, explaining that this particular style, the Sukho-Thai, dated back to the thirteenth century.

Lexa looked around, noticing the inevitable saffron-robed monks all about the place. They were everywhere, but then they were bound to be, she thought, aware that there were numerous wats in the city and the word 'wat' meant monastery.

That evening they dined at the Coronet, one of Bangkok's oldest hotels, and one of the most select. In a romantic setting of music and flowers, of shaded lights nestling among tropical vegetation, they ate a meal of *tempura*—shrimps—followed by *phyathai*, roast chicken with egg-plant salad, and for dessert they had fried bananas marinated in wine and covered with nuts and lashings of cream. Waitresses were in Thai costume and classical Thai dancing was presented while the meal was being served. Afterwards Lexa and Paul strolled in the charming private gardens, among other couples, most of whom were holding hands or walking with arms about each other's waists. All so romantic, thought Lexa, and yet she and her bridegroom were a million miles apart, separated by a memory....

She was glad when it was all over and they were back at

the villa of Koh Kham, yet the memory of the few days following her wedding was for the most part a happy one, mainly because she and Paul had been active the whole time, making visits, cruising on the river, shopping in Gaysorn and the Thieves' Market in Chinatown where Paul bought her an antique bracelet in gold set with star sapphires. They went by car to the virgin jungle and forest lands of Khao Yai and walked by cool mountain streams and waterfalls, climbing on to a plateau to get a view of the spectacular unspoilt scenery of a jungle abounding in wild orchids and other exotic plant life.

But one of the highlights was, for Lexa, a visit to the Temple of the Dawn—Wat Arun, standing high on the bank of the Chao Phya River, its central tower rising to the sky and surrounded by four other towers resting on a series of terraces supported by rows of sculptured demons and angels. Paul had taken her there early in the morning when the five towers, encrusted with multi-coloured Chinese porcelain and glass inlay, sparkled like a myriad flames in the first rays of the rising sun. Niches in the central *prang* showed the green figure of Indra, chief of the Hindu gods, seated on his three-headed elephant. Paul later took her to a gallery high on the central tower where they had a breathtaking view of the river, the Grand Palace and the city and, looking westwards, the rooftops and trees of Thon Buri dissolving into a distant vista of palm trees and paddi-fields.

Lexa had felt closer to her husband on that morning at dawn than at any time before or since. And he, too, seemed near to her, in sympathy with her keen interest, aware of the stirring of her emotions, and in a moment of impulsiveness totally out of character, he had taken her hand in his and pressed it tightly, as if to reassure her, to tell her that at least they were good friends. For herself, the resolve to treat him coolly was forgotten. She loved him too much, desired fervently that he would soon begin to forget his dead wife, that the very awareness of having another wife would become an aid to forgetfulness.

Alacho was delighted at their return, and even more delighted when she was told that her daddy meant to come home every week-end from now on. Alacho had learned this on her own, so it was a surprise to Lexa when she repeated it.

'My daddy loves me now, so he's coming home every Friday and staying till Monday morning!'

'He is?' Lexa's heart became light. If her husband were at home more then surely something deeper than friendship would eventually result.

Nevertheless, every single night when he went to his room she wondered if he drew out the photograph and looked at it, wondered if he ever came near to tears, as he had on that other night when she had seen him with his head in his hands, shoulders heaving.

With her he was always quiet but never short or brusque, as he had been when she was a mere employee, but weeks went by and there was no sign of any change in his attitude, no hint that he was beginning to forget the tragedy that was regarded by Lexa as a barrier to her own happiness. She had optimistically believed at first that she would ask no more from him than he was willing to give, but as time passed she became more and more aware of his attractions, more conscious of what she was missing. She loved him and would willingly have given herself to him whether he loved her or not. She recalled her conviction that, being a normal healthy male, he would naturally be affected by the desires of sex. But he seemed immune even to her presence for most of the time, although at others he appeared to be profoundly aware of her as a woman, looking at her with an expression which she liked to regard as admiration . . . and perhaps desire.

'You're very lovely,' he had said to her one evening when after dinner they were sitting together in the drawing-room listening to records. She was on the couch, her feet tucked up beneath her long, full skirt which trailed along the couch towards the velvet cushions at the end. Her hair was newly-washed, gleaming and a little windblown because they had strolled for ten minutes or so in the garden before settling down to hear the music. She had smiled at his flattery, and her eyes had shone. She wanted to flirt with him, to tempt him while he was in this mood. Her long thick lashes had come down in a little seductive movement and she had said quiveringly,

'Thank you, Paul. I—I've wanted you—you to notice me. . . .' Her voice trailed as she saw him stiffen. Appalled, she failed utterly to understand what had made her voice words like those.

The evening had fallen flat after that, and before an hour was out Lexa was saying goodnight and leaving the room.

She lay awake, listening for him to come up. They had both moved from the bedrooms they had previously occupied, and were now in two adjoining rooms, the communicating door having been locked from the first.

'Just for the sake of the servants,' Paul had said, but as the door was never unlocked Lexa wondered why he had bothered to trouble himself about the servants' gossip. They were bound to gossip anyway, she thought.

She heard him come up; he seemed to stand for a long while without either moving into the room or even closing the door. Eventually, though, the door did close.

Lexa strained her ears for the sound she did not want to hear ... the opening of the top drawer of the cabinet by his bed, the same cabinet which had stood by his bed in the other room he had occupied. If he did open it she failed to hear. But in her imagination she saw him with the picture in his hands, and a flood of resentment swept over her. She knew a fierce stab of jealousy, and a deep desire for her husband, for his arms about her, for his kiss ... and for more.

But a ghost stood in her way, the memory of a dead wife.

Lexa never could decide just when she began to feel cheated. She had told herself that she could wait, that if and when her husband gave her affection she would be satisfied. Now she knew that nothing but his love would satisfy her. She wanted everything from her marriage— love, friendship, children.

And Paul was giving her none of these. True, his manner was friendly for the most part, but often he would brood, become morose, and she felt sure he was thinking of the past, and of the wife he had lost.

With Alacho he was the tender loving father, and Lexa would stand sometimes, watching them playing with the dog on the lawn, and she would feel that at least in one way she had succeeded in what she had set out to do.

If only she could succeed in making Paul notice her—— No, not merely notice her, for he had done that already, but if only by some miracle she could make him love her.

She recalled those occasions when he *had* noticed her. His eyes had held admiration, but almost instantly a frown had touched his brow, as if he were feeling guilty that his interest had become fixed upon another woman. He had at times appeared to be fighting something strong within himself, and as she reflected on this Lexa's spirits rose. Surely if he saw something attractive in her then she was part way to her objective. After all, she had not made any appreciable effort to win his love; she had been friendly, had run the house efficiently, had been a good mother to Alacho, but very seldom had she gone out of her way to attract her husband in the way she so desperately wanted to attract him.

She would try to rectify that, she resolved, in spite of the rebuff she had received as a result of her one frail attempt, when she had hesitantly admitted that she had wanted him to notice her. She must be far more subtle than that, she decided, yet the idea was vague simply because she had no idea how to begin.

However, the following Saturday evening seemed a good time to make her first attempt, because Paul was in one of his most pleasant moods, having played all afternoon on the sands with Alacho, while Lexa watched from her comfortable lounger which one of the servants had brought out on to the shore. Paul had swum for a while, then helped Alacho to make a huge sand castle. After that they had played beach ball, and in this Lexa was persuaded to join.

'Come on, lazybones!' Alacho had cried. 'Daddy, make her come and play!'

'Up you get,' he had said, and it was in effect an order which Lexa had immediately obeyed.

And later, after they had all had tea on the terrace, and Alacho was put to bed, Paul had suggested a stroll in the gardens before dinner. Lexa was happy walking by his side, vitally aware of his nearness, of the magic of the atmosphere, the romance of the tropical setting.

The sun had gone down in a blaze of glory against an eggshell sky; the flaring colours were replaced by purple and grey and smoky blue. Shadows among the palms were mysterious, stimulating emotions profound and indescribable. Paul was quiet, but there was a strange friendliness in his silence. Lexa felt that if she had had the courage to take his hand she would not have been repulsed. But she did not have the courage, and it was with a little sigh that she was admitting it a short while later as she dressed for dinner. She had showered, then used a tempting talc and perfume on her body. The dress she had chosen was of orchid blue which brought out the colour of her eyes. It was of Edwardian style, tight-bodiced to accentuate her curves, and full-skirted in tantalising folds that swayed out as she walked. Her hair had been washed and styled that morning; it shone like pure gold but the front, where it had been bleached by the sun, was the pure fine colour of platinum.

She stayed for a long moment, after she was ready, surveying herself in the mirror, faint shadows of doubt in her eyes but hope in her heart. Surely Paul would be struck by what he saw. Lexa wondered about his wife, Sally, and thought she must have looked very beautiful to him when she was dressed something like this, for she had features that were sheer perfection, hair that formed a glorious halo, eyes that were large and honest. . . . What a handsome pair they must have made, when Paul was without that scar. Lexa fell to imagining their wedding, comparing it with her own. Paul had worn a dark lounge suit; she had worn a white linen suit. No fairytale dress for her, with veil and orange blossom and flowers. Tears stung her eyes and an ache caught her throat. The wedding of Paul and Sally would have been a very different affair—— Lexa cut her thoughts angrily. She was being morbid, dwelling on an event that was long past, that had been no concern of hers and never could be. She had her life, her husband, and the future. She intended to live!

Paul was in the drawing-room when she went in and to her intense satisfaction she saw that he had noticed her, so much so that his eyes remained on her for far longer than was necessary.

'You look charming,' he said softly. 'I haven't seen that dress before, have I?'

She shook her head, a smile on her lips. She came further into the room and stood near him, glancing up, a sort of gentle appeal in her manner.

'No. I haven't worn it before.'

'The colour suits you admirably. You must wear more of it.' He flicked a hand, indicating a chair. 'What can I get you to drink?'

She told him and he poured it for her. She watched him covertly, noticing the immaculate cut of his white linen suit, the jacket draped and cut away to reveal the frilled shirt of Thai silk. Turning, he smiled, brought her the drink which he placed on a small table at her elbow.

'You smell nice,' he said, ending the short sentence abruptly and swinging away towards the record player. Lexa sighed, aware that he was angry with himself for giving her more than perfunctory attention. She suddenly knew a little access of anger, wondering if it were his intention to keep the gulf wide open for the rest of their married life. Well, she would not let him keep it open! She had very successfully managed to close the gulf which had existed between him and his daughter, and now she had every intention of doing her utmost to close the gulf existing between him and his wife!

The record was called 'Softly Sentimental' and was a medley of love songs of three or four decades ago. The strains came through, tender, filling the room, matching the candlelight and the flowers. And the same atmosphere prevailed in the dining-room, to which they went about ten minutes later. Speakers had been installed high on the walls, and the music, playing now from a tape, added magic and romance to the setting of elegance and good taste.

Paul drew out her chair; she deliberately brushed his chin with her hair. If he smelled the perfume he made no comment, but when he sat down opposite to her Lexa noticed an odd, half-frowning expression on his face. His eyes found hers and stayed there for a profound moment before moving, to her forehead, then down to her lips and her chin. She noticed that nerve pulsating in his throat, against the scar which seemed in the last few seconds to have gained a depth of colour.

After the first course was finished she said,

'Will you dance with-me, Paul? I adore this tune! It always makes me want to dance.'

He gave a small start at the unexpected invitation, but to her surprise he rose at once and took her in his arms. They danced for no more than a few moments, but Lexa was happy. He stood with her for a space, looking down into her shining eyes.

'That was most enjoyable, Lexa,' he admitted. 'We'll do it between each course.'

A smile curved her lips.

'It's—sort of—of intimate, isn't it?' She held her breath, regretting the words that had escaped unbidden. His mouth tightened, but when he spoke it was gently, with that attractive brogue coming through.

'Yes, I suppose it is. The tune was haunting.'

They ate the second course in silence, listening to the music, then when the servant appeared they rose again, and this time it was a waltz: *Falling in love with love,* and the strains were soft and tender, the candlelight golden; the perfume of flowers filled the room. Lexa felt heady with emotions heightened by the romantic atmosphere, by the closeness of her husband's body and the strength of his arm about her. Instinctively she strained her own body to him, diffident and yet at the same time urged by a desire she could not control. Physically she wanted him; her love was like a deluge swamping every other feeling, fierce and demanding.

She could almost have asked him to make love to her.

It was an anticlimax when they eventually sat down to the dessert course; Lexa had never felt less like eating. Paul's manner was cool, polite, suave. Resentment rose as a direct result of her awakened senses; she knew that feeling of being cheated. She was a bride and yet little more to her husband than she had been when she was a mere nanny to his child. His eyes caught hers; she saw them narrow, noticed the frown that touched his forehead. His lips were tight. A flood of embarrassment swept away her desire as she realised that he had guessed at her feelings, that he knew of her desire.... Colour rushed into her cheeks and resentment rose, mingling with the humiliation that now filled her. For him to have guessed.... And yet wasn't that what she had aimed for? Yes—but she had not wanted him to react like this! Not by any means. She had wanted him to respond in a very different way.

That sense of being cheated was growing to the sort of proportions that threatened to affect her patience and, as a result, her actions. For suddenly she wanted to have it out with him, to demand to know whether she was to be a wife in name only for the rest of their lives together. She wanted to point out that she had rights, to remind him that *he* had rights too and that if he were to decide to assert his right then she would have no alternative than to submit to his demands.

She heard his voice, soft, unfathomable.

'What are you thinking about, Lexa?'

Her eyes were dark and angry.

'It doesn't matter.'

'Obviously it does,' he contradicted, 'for otherwise you wouldn't be as deeply affected as you are.'

'You appear to know,' she returned shortly.

'I know that something is affecting you——'

'It doesn't matter,' she said again, rudely interrupting him and bringing a glint to his eyes.

'You've changed dramatically in the last few minutes,' he commented.

'Perhaps.'

'There must be a reason.'

She shrugged and picked up her spoon and fork.

'You wouldn't be interested.' This time there was a distinct note of bitterness in her tone that could not possibly escape him.

'I believe I would be exceedingly interested,' he argued, tight-lipped.

She began to eat her sweet.

'Shall we change the subject, Paul?'

'If you wish. The present one appears to be distasteful to us both.'

Startled, she stopped eating to stare at him.

'It's obvious that you've guessed even more than I supposed.' She had not meant to be so open, but now that the words were out she had no regrets. Let the matter come to a head. It was time it did.

'It was not difficult to guess,' returned Paul quietly. He was so aloof and dignified; Lexa felt small and inferior, stung by the knowledge that she was to receive a reprimand. 'Your very attitude reveals much. I'd be blind if I didn't see that you're dissatisfied with your lot.' He paused a moment, staring into her hot face. 'You want more from the marriage than I promised.' A statement spoken with a stern admonishing inflection that made her squirm. 'Suddenly you've decided you have rights. Perhaps it's that you want children——' He shook his head. 'You knew, Lexa, when you made that contract with me, what you were letting yourself in for. At the time you accepted what I offered and gave no indication that you would ever want more. You'll abide by your decision,' he continued sternly. 'I want no more of this nonsense, understand?'

Even more colour flooded her cheeks at his words, and the manner of their utterance. So arrogantly superior; the master speaking to his servant! Perhaps that was a slight exaggeration, but she was so furious she could have picked up her dessert plate and thrown the contents into his face. Instead, she rose from the chair, bade him a stiff goodnight, and swept from the room.

She was undressed and about to pull her nightgown over her head when she heard the key being turned in the lock of the communicating door. It was flung wide open and Paul entered without uttering a word. Blushing furiously, Lexa fumbled with the nightdress, getting her hands entangled in its folds and frills and cursing herself for her clumsiness.

'What—what do you want?' she demanded when at last she had her body covered. 'If you expect me to apologise for leaving you at dinner then——'

'I haven't come for an apology,' he interrupted in a very soft tone. 'It's something different altogether ...

something that will obviously meet with your approval.'

She stared, aware of a nerve-twisting tension within her, of the blood rushing to her heart, causing it to hammer against her ribs.

'Something—something—different. . . .' Her throat was dry suddenly and she found speech difficult. 'If you—mean—mean——?'

'That's exactly what I mean.' There was a sort of mild and tranquil contempt about his manner as he stood there, just inside her room, one hand resting on the back of a velvet-coloured chair, the other thrust deep into his jacket pocket. Tall and overpowering, with the scar livid against the pulsating nerve, he seemed so formidable as to be terrifying and Lexa wished with all her heart that she had used more control at hiding her feelings. 'You have rights,' he went on presently, 'and you've indicated that you ought to be able to assert them——'

'You would assert *your* rights,' she broke in, too embarrassed to let him continue, and at the same time saying the first thing that came into her head. 'Men can, but women——'

'In these times of equality it seems reasonable for a woman to be in a position to assert her rights.'

She looked at him for a space, then swung away, to stand by the window. It was open and the silken net billowed in, swirling around her, wraith-like and seductive, while the soft gentle breeze teased her hair, sending it about her face.

'Please go,' she managed at last, marvelling that her voice was calm and steady. 'I'm sure this little scene's as embarrassing to you as it is to me.'

'Do I appear embarrassed?' He glanced over her, a sort of disdainful indifference in his eyes. And yet. . . . As she stared Lexa felt sure that all this was a pose for her bene-

fit, that he was affected just as she was, that if he did
stay and make love to her it would not be entirely because *she* had wanted it. However, she had no intention
that he should stay; she did not want it like this—as if
he were doing her a favour, pandering to her wishes. 'I
assure you, my dear,' he was saying, 'that I'm in no way
embarrassed. We're man and wife; it's not unnatural that
we should share a bed——'

'We are not sharing a bed!'

'I assure you we are.' He moved, slowly and—to
Lexa's rather warped imagination—menacingly, towards
her. She was unable to back further and she just stood
there, body trembling, a sudden shake of her head de-
noting her objection to what he was about to do. He
merely smiled sardonically and on reaching her drew
her forward, protestingly, but his was the sort of easy
strength that defeated at once any struggles she had begun to make. His arms crushed her; his kiss, fierce and
savage, was a revelation for she had not thought him
capable of such violent passion.

It lasted for what seemed an eternity; she was carried
reluctantly through the stages of his ardour, his hands
caressing her throat, her shoulders, her breasts. She felt
the narrow straps of the nightgown being slid
from her shoulders, felt one warm hand along her spine,
provocative, enticing.... Her emotions, merely smoul-
dering at first, were ignited by his, then suddenly they
were on fire and she was responding, straining to him,
thrilling as his hand slid lower and lower down her spine.
She was lifted—swung right up into his arms—and
placed on the bed.

'I won't be long,' he promised, staring down into eyes
hazed and dreamy with yearning. 'Don't get into bed.
Stay on top—it's nicer that way.' He turned to the bed

lamp, brought down the shade until the room was bathed in a subtle amber-rose glow which reflected on the curtains as, after closing the window, he drew them together, using the heavy cord hanging at the side. He swung around but stood still, looking at her across the room. She lay still, breathless and contented, even though at the back of her mind she was aware of his contempt. It would not always be so, she thought optimistically. He would learn to love her; she would make him!

'Don't go to sleep,' he said with a touch of amused satire as he came across the room. Bending, he patted her cheek—a little harder and rougher than was necessary, she thought. 'I'll be with you in a couple of minutes.'

He went to the door, passed through it but left it wide open. And, true to his word, he was back with her in a couple of minutes. . . .

CHAPTER TEN

DURING the next few weeks Lexa found herself desperately trying to quell the fear that was gradually spreading over her, for although her relationship with her husband was now normal, she was constantly aware of the tension that was always there when he came to her. And at times he as so cold and remote that she despaired of ever managing to come really close to him. She had a formidable barrier to scale—the memory that still seemed to haunt him.

He said one day, when they were on the sands, watching Alacho playing with a child of her own age, the daughter of a visitor to the island,

'You're still not happy, are you, Lexa?'

She shook her head and answered frankly,

'No, Paul,' and for a moment she hesitated about saying what was in her mind. But she did say it, because lately she had decided not to hide anything but her love. 'Your attitude, Paul, is so often cold and distant.' Another pause; the tears filled her eyes and she made no attempt to conceal them. 'Your concern with the past is too achingly noticeable. . . .' She stopped, slowly, and brushed a hand across her eyes. 'Have—have we made a mistake?' Her eyes pleaded for him to deny that they had made a mistake, but she was disappointed. He merely took on a brooding expression which developed into an abstract look which brought a heaviness to her heart. She was fighting a losing battle, she thought, and if it had not been for Alacho she would have asked him for her freedom. Again she said what was in her mind. 'The memory of your wife, Paul—will it be with you for ever?'

He looked at her, his eyes roving her scantily-clad figure.

'I'd rather not talk about it, Lexa.'

Anger mingled with the pain; it brought a sparkle to her eyes.

'I'm your wife now,' she said. 'You ought not to have even contemplated a second marriage, feeling the way you did.'

'You knew how I felt. I told you the memory would always hurt. You accepted the situation when you agreed to marry me——' He broke off shortly and turned away from her. 'Sally and I made vows to one another—that we would be true for the whole of our lives, that we would never love another.' The sombre inflection in his voice seemed more like regret than resignation. 'I firmly believe that if she had been widowed she would have remained like that for the rest of her life.'

'Would you have wanted her to?' Lexa looked straight at him, aware that he had said, only a moment ago, that he would rather not talk about his late wife. 'Would you have been so selfish as to have expected her to remain single for the rest of her life?'

He frowned heavily at her and became lost in thought.

'No,' he admitted at last, 'I wouldn't.'

'Neither would she have expected you to live a lonely life.'

'There's logic in what you say.'

'But as you're not in love with me my logic doesn't fit the present situation. Had you waited you might eventually have fallen in love with someone—— No, don't interrupt me, Paul! People do get over tragedies, you know that. And they marry again and are happy. But you didn't wait long enough; you married for convenience, because of Mrs Sharman and her ownership of part of the property. You decided to marry me, believing we could continue as near strangers for the rest of our lives——' She broke off, nerves so tensed that she found herself suppressing hysterical laughter. 'It's funny,' she went on shrilly, 'funny and absurd! Two people, healthy and young—living together and yet not together! Where was your intelligence——!'

'Stop it!' he thundered. 'Pull yourself together! You accepted the contract as it stood. I've met you more than half way and yet you're still not satisfied.'

'Thanks for meeting me half way, as you term it! In future, then, you can keep to your own side of that door! And as soon as Alacho is old enough to look after herself it's goodbye! Get that—and remember it!'

Her voice vibrated with anger but she did manage to keep it low, for she had an idea that Paul had come very close to striking her—if she had been unable to control that laughter he certainly would have done.

It was not laughter that affected her as she rose and hurried from him, but tears, bitter tears of regret that she had allowed the situation to get out of hand like that. Matters were worsened by it and now she greatly feared that even friendliness would fade from their relationship. He did not follow and it was dinner time before they met again, a meal eaten in total silence, each of them brooding over their respective hurts.

It came as a shock, therefore, when, just after she had entered her bedroom, Paul knocked lightly and entered. She had been out on the verandah for the past half hour; he had apparently gone straight to his room because he was in his dressing-gown, and he had obviously showered and washed his hair, for it was damp and shining, with tendrils lying on his forehead.

Lexa said sharply,

'What do you want? I told you to keep to your side of that door.'

'You——!' His eyes smouldered and Lexa was suddenly afraid of him. She had witnessed his ruthlessness with his child and she had no wish to have it directed against herself. 'I don't allow my wife to speak to me like that!'

My wife.... So seldom had he called her that, and now he had done so it had to be in anger.

'Why have you come, Paul?' she asked him quietly.

He looked at her, his eyes moving from her face to the lovely evening gown she wore, a slim-fitting creation which clung seductively to her lovely curves.

'That,' he said with the merest hint of satire, 'is a strange question to ask.'

She was pale but composed as she said,

'I meant it, Paul, when I told you that our—er—marital relationship was at an end.'

His straight black brows lifted a fraction. He thrust a hand into his pocket and leant against the jamb of the door, his eyes never leaving her face.

'You began something, Lexa, which I'm not at present willing to terminate.'

She coloured at the way he spoke.

'It would be immoral to continue,' she protested.

'Isn't it rather late to think of that?' he asked, smiling faintly.

'Late or not, I have thought of it.' She stared unwaveringly at him. 'I'm not willing to be that kind of wife,' she told him firmly.

'What kind of wife?'

She sighed impatiently.

'You want me just as a convenience.'

His grey eyes widened.

'I was not aware that the approach was mine in the first place,' was his rather dry reminder.

'I don't see that it matters. What is gone is gone and it's the future only that concerns me now. As I said to you out there on the sands, I shall leave you once Alacho is able to do without me.'

'That's years from now. We must live meanwhile. We were getting along fine until today——'

He stopped as she shook her head.

'We were living normally in one way, but there was neither warmth nor intimacy in our relationship.' She lifted her face and he saw that there were tears in her eyes. 'You're incapable of giving me warmth, Paul, so you might as well admit it. I myself have become re-signed and my plans are made. I'll stay while Alacho needs me and after that we shall have a divorce.'

'You speak very casually of divorce.'

'It happens to be a casual business these days.'

He said unexpectedly,

'Come here, Lexa.'

She looked at him, startled, a fluttering sensation in the pit of her stomach. Did he intend to take her by force?

'No—I w-won't,' she returned, shaking her head. 'I've asked you to go.'

It was Paul's turn to shake his head.

'I'm not in the mood to leave,' he admitted frankly. 'I came here to make love to my wife and I intend to do just that.'

She stepped back as he moved forward, shades of fear and distress in her lovely eyes.

'Please go,' she begged, taking another step backwards.

'I said ... come here.' He pointed to a spot close to his feet. 'I'm not leaving,' he assured her, 'so you might as well obey me.'

She had not often seen him so stern, or so arrogantly masterful. His chin was rigid, his eyes narrowed and resolute. Lexa shook her head again even while knowing that she would obey him in the end.

'I asked you to leave me alone——'

'Come here!' He meant her to do his bidding and automatically she stopped in her backward progress. Her eyes filled, but tears seemed to have no effect on him as he added imperiously, 'I'm waiting, Lexa!'

For another brief moment she hesitated before, with a little quivering gesture of resignation, she went slowly towards him. He took both her hands, and she thought afterwards that he would have been gentle with her had she gone to him willingly, but protest was strong within her, and resentment of his mastery high. She stiffened first, then struggled as he made to fetch her body close to his. She managed to escape him because he had not expected any resistance. When it came it seemed to incense him; she saw his mouth compress, his nostrils flare—and the scar was dark crimson and swollen. She shuddered, recoiling from him, her heart racing madly. His brow darkened ominously and swiftly she was captured again and brought up roughly against his steel-hard frame.

'This was begun for your pleasure,' he snarled, 'and it will continue for mine!'

'Let me go—oh, please——' The rest was smothered beneath the savage cruelty of his mouth. She tried to struggle again, but desisted as she realised she was gaining nothing but bruises. His lips were ruthless in their demands, forcing her own lips apart, bruising them, possessing them with a sort of primitive intensity. This was the side of him she had suspected but never expected to see, for usually he was so calm and self-possessed, more than able to control his passions. But not now; anger had taken over to the exclusion of control, of pity, of respect. Lexa became limp in his arms, docilely accepting his mastery, his complete domination of her. She was inert as he manipulated the fastener of her dress and let it fall to the floor; she was incapable of protest when other, daintier clothing was removed. And eventually she stood naked before him, watching his eyes examining her body, feeling his exploring hands. But she was crying quietly when he lifted her and carried her across the room. He laid her down, his eyes narrowed with an unfathomable expression. His savagery seemed to have evaporated; his hands were gentle as they smoothed the hair away from her face.

'Why did you resist me?' The harsh demand in his voice was at complete variance with his gentleness of only seconds ago. 'In future, obey me! It will be far more comfortable for you!'

He was untying the cord of his dressing-gown; the pyjama coat was open to reveal the dark hairs on his chest. Lexa closed her eyes, and kept them closed as he lay down beside her. His hands took her breasts, cupping them, caressing them before his mouth explored, hungrily, voraciously. She wanted to resist his attraction, his tempting finesse, but to her shame she knew an exquisite sensation of fear and expectancy, of fluttering nerves, excitedly out of all control. Nothing mattered but this moment, even though she knew for sure that there would be no tenderness in her husband's lovemaking, since he considered he was taking her against her will, asserting his arrogant mastery, his complete superiority over her. He was not to know that the effort of trying to resist had done nothing more than heighten the sensation of her own longing for him. She saw his face above hers, serene and savage in the argent shaft of moonlight that penetrated the room, for on this occasion Paul had left the curtains open wide, and had snapped off the bedside lamp. The light was vibrant and crystalline, causing the scar to appear almost white. It seemed a more fearful disfigurement than ever before ... and yet, strangely, it was not in the least repulsive to her. Her love was such that she saw no blemishes, and even as she gave of her all she could lift a finger to touch the scar, gently, caressingly.

The following morning Paul had risen before Lexa was awake. He had gone for a swim, Maria told her when she arrived in the breakfast room to find he was not there.

'Shall I serve your breakfast?' asked Maria, smiling.

'No, I'll wait.' Lexa felt uneasy without knowing why. She sensed a sort of drama in the air, which seemed quite absurd, seeing that she was all alone in here.

Paul's face was set and dark when eventually he put in an appearance.

'You shouldn't have waited for me,' he told Lexa curtly as he took possession of a chair opposite to her. 'There was no need.'

'I wanted to,' she said quietly, that sense of uneasiness growing alongside a sort of breathless waiting ... for what?

It was as they began on the eggs and bacon that he said,

'Would you be happier if I stayed in Bangkok?'

She looked at him, startled in spite of the conviction

that something dramatic was about to happen.

'You want to stay there, in the hotel?'

'I feel it would solve some problems.'

'Of you and me—of our relationship?' A terrible dejection was slowly creeping over her. 'Is there really any need for us to live separate lives, Paul?' He said nothing and after a space she added, 'You feel that I want more than you're willing to give—that's it, isn't it?'

'You're not willing to abide by the bargain you made.' Although his voice was tight and almost harsh, Lexa had the strange conviction that these words were not what he really wanted to voice.

'I admit that I now feel I want more from our marriage than mere friendship,' she said at last. 'I'm young, Paul, and I want children. It's not unnatural, is it?' Her voice was low and pleading. She hoped it did not reveal the love that was in her heart. 'I said that you find it impossible to give me warmth, and I suppose in a way I understand. Your late wife——'

'We'll leave her out of it,' he snapped. 'We were talking about us—you and me—not the past.'

She swallowed, trying to dislodge the painful little lump in her throat.

'If you want to live in Bangkok,' she managed at last, 'then do so. It's your decision entirely, I expect you'll do what pleases you, so this discussion is not going to get us anywhere.' She thought of Alacho, and the new and intimate relationship that had developed between her and her father, as a direct result of Lexa's efforts. 'Alacho will miss you,' she just had to say, a catch in her voice.

Paul nodded, frowning heavily.

'I shall miss her,' he admitted, a sigh on his lips. He looked at his wife across the table. 'You meant what you said when you threatened to leave me, once Alacho's old enough to look after herself?'

There was a slight hesitation before Lexa said,

'What would there be for me here, Paul?' She looked down at her plate. '*You* would already have left *me*, remember.'

'I certainly hadn't contemplated a complete break,' said Paul swiftly. 'I shall come here at intervals, naturally.'

'At intervals.' The bitterness in her voice was bound to come through to him and he stared at her in the strangest way, stared as if he had learned something he wanted to learn.

'You haven't answered my question,' he said slowly, his grey eyes intently fixed upon her face. 'Do you mean to leave here when Alacho's grown up?'

She said, after another hesitation,

'As the answer is by no means urgent, shall we leave it for the present?'

'But I want to know. It's important——' He stopped and turned, a swift frown gathering on his forehead. Alacho danced into the room, clad in her dressing-gown.

'I'm awake, Lexa! I want to get up!'

A small silence ensued, while Paul and Lexa stared at one another, each wishing the other's thoughts could be read. But Alacho's entrance had not only eased the situation but had made further discussion impossible. Paul remained silent, but Lexa laughed rather shakily as she said,

'You are up, silly! Why aren't you washed and dressed?'

'I thought you'd want to bath me.'

'I'll come up and do it.' Lexa half rose from her chair, but Paul told her to sit down.

'You're too early, Alacho,' he said, but slipped an arm about her all the same, as she came and stood beside him. 'Lexa hasn't had her breakfast yet.'

'Can I have mine here, Daddy? I think I'm getting too old to have it in the nursery—and anyway, I don't like it now that Lexa doesn't have it with me. She used to do, before you got married. Now she has to have it with you.'

'She doesn't have to,' he corrected, his eyes flickering briefly towards his wife as if he wished to note her expression. 'She chooses to.'

Lexa coloured and glanced away, so that she failed to notice that her husband nodded.

'Because she likes to sit with you,' declared Alacho. 'But I want to have mine with you as well. It's better when there's three of us—like at lunch when you're at home, Daddy. And another thing——' Alacho wagged a finger at him, giggling triumphantly as she managed to pull it away before he caught it. 'I ought to be allowed to stay up and have dinner with you and Lexa! I'm nearly seven, remember!'

'An age when a box on the ear wouldn't come amiss! No, my child, you will not be allowed to stay up for dinner! Sit down if you must, and Lexa will give you something to eat, but don't make a practice of interrupting her and me at this time. We enjoy beginning the day together ... and ending it together.'

Lexa, her heart pounding, said bewilderedly,

'Paul—I don't understand—I d-don't know what you're saying—— What I'm trying to tell you is——'

'Too difficult?' His eyes had softened miraculously, and a smile tinged with tender amusement curved his mouth. 'Save it, dear,' he advised. 'There really is no great hurry, is there?'

'No....' She shook her head dazedly. She still did not understand, but she did know that a miracle had happened and as a result of it her heart was singing and a great wave of happiness was flooding over her.

Impatient as she was to find herself alone with Paul, Lexa was to have to wait until dinner-time. It was Saturday and she had her usual hair appointment in town; no sooner had she returned than Paul was called to the telephone by one of his managers and was kept there for over an hour and a half. Alacho did not help. Usually she would play in the garden for part of the time, with one of the gardeners and the dog, or she would wander on to the beach to find some other child who might be there. But not today. She wanted to be with Lexa, and with her daddy when he came from the phone, so the three of them were together on the beach for most of the afternoon, after which Lexa gave Alacho her tea, bathed her and, after putting her to bed, spent almost an hour reading to her before there was any sign that the child was ready for sleep.

But at last Lexa was in the bedroom, changing for the evening meal. She chose a white gossamer dress with many underskirts, a very tight-fitting bodice and long voluminous sleeves, transparent to reveal the bangles she wore, Thai-style, on both her arms. A diamond clip given her by Paul enhanced the golden, ethereal halo of her hair, and matching drops adorned her ears. Her hand trembled as she manipulated the perfume spray— in fact, every nerve seemed to be quivering with excitement and expectation. She heard her husband in the next room and seemed momentarily to panic, an urge to escape assailing her so that she fled to the door, opened it, and went down to the sitting-room, where music was already playing, where candles burned and flower perfumes filled the air.

The window was wide open to the breeze, and the scene outside was one of peace and solemn tranquillity, although there was movement and colour, with the breeze rippling through the trees and the crystal spray of the fountains glistening in the lights from the house, rainbow-coloured one moment, silver the next. From the dome of the tropical sky the mysterious purple darkness pressed down, star-spangled, moon-flushed. Across the silent sea a mist clung to the horizon, distorting the skyline, but through it came the lights of a ship riding the waves, smooth, haunting, so very far away.

Lexa turned, heartstrings going tight as Paul came into the room—so tall and masculine, dressed to perfection in pearl-grey linen with a mauve frilled shirt of Thai silk. She glanced into his eyes, shyness holding back both smile and words. She noticed the scar—pale, less pronounced than she had ever seen it. She suddenly knew that time would make it fade, knew that at first it had been much much more disfiguring than it was today.

'Lexa....' Soft the tone as Paul came towards her. 'I've waited all day for this moment.' He held forth his hands and gladly she swept towards him, placing hers confidently on his open palms. His fingers closed, caressed, then one hand was brought to his lips. 'You love me,' he said simply. 'Why didn't you let me know?'

She looked up at him, eyes misted.

'How do you know I love you?' was all she could find to say, perhaps because the question had been with her all through the day. For it was plain that, somehow, he had discovered that she cared.

'The terrible bitterness in your voice when you spoke.

after I said I would return here at intervals. But there were other signs, darling. You hesitated when I asked if you really meant to leave me; the second time I asked was after you'd shown that bitterness—there's always a reason for bitterness, Lexa,' he went on, digressing for a moment. 'I seemed to grasp, in a flash of enlightenment, that your bitterness meant that there was love in your heart for me. There could be no other reason for it.' He paused, looking tenderly at her, aware that she was still bewildered but aware also that she now knew that he loved her. He began to explain, reverting for a space to what he had been saying before about his wanting to know if she had meant it when she said she would leave him. 'You prevaricated the second time, Lexa, but I knew you'd never leave me——' He stopped and drew her into his arms. 'And there could be only one reason why you'd never leave me, couldn't there?'

She nodded, too full to speak, and he bent his head to kiss her quivering lips. 'I've been learning to love you,' he confessed. 'For some time I realised that you had an attraction for me, but always was the thought of Sally, of what she had suffered, of the vows we made to one another. I felt disloyal even in admiring you, in thinking to myself: she looks pretty today in that colour, or on other occasions, admiring your figure, especially if you were out there on the sands, with very little on.' He stopped and smiled, because she was blushing slightly and plucking unconsciously at the lapel of his coat. 'Then later, when you wanted me—— Darling, don't be embarrassed, because there's no need to be. When you wanted me—well, I can admit now that I wanted you too, so it was not as one-sided as I so callously tried to make out it was. But again I felt that disloyalty. I hated myself for the enjoyment of possessing you, and yet I was fast realising that I'd tasted something that I could not easily give up.'

He paused and Lexa spoke at last, reminding him that he was in fact ready to bring an end to the relationship that had developed between them.

'You suggested leaving here and living at the hotel,' she added accusingly.

'I felt, after last night, when you obviously hated the idea of my making love to you, that the best way for us both would be to live apart for most of the time....' His voice began to trail as he noticed her expression. 'What is it, dear?'

She was suppressing laughter.

'Oh, Paul, how very blind you are! Did you really believe I hated your making love to me?'

His eyes flickered.

'Last night you did—most definitely! Why, you fought me. You ordered me to leave, then begged me to do so. But by that time there was no drawing back for me. I was a brute to you, dearest——' Lexa stopped him by bringing a gentle hand to his lips.

'Whatever impression you got last night, Paul, I didn't hate your making love to me; I never have because, you see, I've loved you for a long time.'

'I can see it now,' he told her with a hint of regret. 'How I must have hurt you—— And yet, Lexa dear, I'd come to the point where I no longer resented your not wanting to keep to the terms of the agreement. I must have been crazy to believe we could live like that! As you so wisely remarked, we're two normal, healthy people, and we're man and wife.' He looked down into her eyes, love and tenderness giving great depth to his. 'We were bound to fall in love, weren't we, sweetheart?'

She nodded in agreement, but it was an automatic

gesture and when she spoke it was to say,

'I was bound to fall in love with you, Paul, but you.... I was afraid, terribly afraid of—of the memory....'

'I did say, once, that it was hurting less and less as time went by. It doesn't hurt now, darling. You do believe me?' He was anxious and it showed in his gaze.

'I do believe you,' she reassured him, clinging to him and lifting her lips to his. He kissed her, tenderly, passionately, and for a long while the only sounds in the room were the music and the whisper of the breeze as it drifted through the window. 'When did it begin to fade?' Lexa never meant to ask a question like that; it came out unbidden.

'Looking back,' he mused, 'I realise that the pain began to fade as soon as I began to come close to my child. I'd resented Alacho, had stubbornly considered her to blame—indirectly, I was ready to own—for my inability to save Sally, but as you so rightly pointed out, what happened was never any blame of Alacho's. It was fate and I began to accept it—due entirely to you, my dearest. Had you not come into my life it would have still been one of purgatory and hopelessness ... and hatred of my child.'

Lexa clung to him and for a while she felt too full to speak, but eventually she did break the silence, to say simply,

'And now, darling Paul, your life is happy.'

He nodded; she saw that nerve move, but not with the violent pulsating rhythm she had seen on so many occasions before. She knew that within him now there was only peace, and contentment, that the past was rapidly being forgotten and it was the future with which his thoughts were now concerned. She had won, bringing him from his misery to joy, from a pernicious darkness to the sun's healing light. There were no words to convey what was in her heart, and Paul seemed to understand, for he drew her slender body to him, embracing it tenderly, reverently, and sought her lips with the same tenderness, closing his mouth on hers in a long and loving kiss.

The Mills & Boon Rose is the Rose of Romance

Every month there are ten new titles to choose from — ten new stories about people falling in love, people you want to read about, people in exciting, far away places. Choose Mills & Boon. It's your way of relaxing.

December's titles are:

TEMPLE OF THE DAWN by *Anne Hampson*
Lexa lost her heart to Paul Mansell — but his heart belonged, as it always would, to his beautiful dead wife Sally ...

MY DARLING SPITFIRE by *Rosemary Carter*
The only way Siane could join her fiancé on a remote game reserve was to go in the company of the *maddening* André Connors!

KONA WINDS by *Janet Dailey*
Happy in her teaching job in Hawaii, Julie then met her pupil's grim half-brother ...

BOOMERANG BRIDE by *Margaret Pargeter*
Four years ago, when Vicki was expecting her husband Wade's child, he had thrown her out. So why was he now forcing her to return?

SAVAGE INTERLUDE by *Carole Mortimer*
James St Just was Kate's half-brother, but Damien Savage didn't know that, and he had jumped to all the wrong conclusions ...

THE JASMINE BRIDE by *Daphne Clair*
Rachel didn't think it mattered that she was so much younger than Damon Curtis — but she was also very much more inexperienced ...

CHAMPAGNE SPRING by *Margaret Rome*
The arrogant Marquis de la Roque thought the worst of Chantal and her brother — but she was determined to prove him wrong!

DEVIL ON HORSEBACK by *Elizabeth Graham*
Joanne went as housekeeper to Alex Harper — but he was convinced that she was only yet another candidate for the position of his wife ...

PRINCE OF DARKNESS by *Susanna Firth*
After five years' separation from her husband Elliott, Cassie was just about getting over it when Elliott turned up again — as her boss.

COUNTRY COUSIN by *Jacqueline Gilbert*
Eleanor liked most of the Mansel family. What a pity she couldn't feel the same way about one of them, the uncompromising Edward ...

If you have difficulty in obtaining any of these books from your local paperback retailer, write to:

Mills and Boon Reader Service
P.O. Box No 236, Thornton Road, Croydon, Surrey CR9 3RU.

189

Bring back the age of romance this Christmas

Masquerade
Historical Romances

Intrigue ✳ *excitement* ✳ *romance*

Eight of your favourite titles in two
specially-produced gift packs.

THE RUNAWAYS *Julia Herbert*
ELEANOR AND THE MARQUIS *Jane Wilby*
A ROSE FOR DANGER *Marguerite Bell*
THE SECRET OF VAL VERDE *Judith Polley*

PURITAN WIFE *Elizabeth de Guise*
THE KING'S SHADOW *Judith Polley*
THE FORTUNE – HUNTER *Julia Herbert*
FRANCESCA *Valentina Luellen*

**UNITED KINGDOM £1.95 net per pack
REP. OF IRELAND £2.15 per pack**

Still available from
your local paperback
retailer.

The Mills & Boon Rose is the Rose of Romance

Look for the Mills & Boon Rose next month

BED OF GRASS *by Janet Dailey*
Judd Prescott had been the reason for Valerie leaving home.
Now she was back, but Judd still didn't know what that
reason had been . . .

WINTER WEDDING *by Betty Neels*
Professor Renier Jurres-Romeijn regarded Emily as a 'prim
miss'. So it wasn't surprising that he so obviously preferred
her lively sister Louise.

DANGEROUS DECEPTION *by Lilian Peake*
Anona Willis was engaged to the forceful Shane Brodie — but
he had admitted that he had no staying power where women
were concerned . . .

FEVER *by Charlotte Lamb*
The attraction between Sara Nichols and Nick Rawdon was
immediate — but somehow Sara could never clear up the
misunderstanding about her stepbrother Greg.

SWEET HARVEST *by Kerry Allyne*
Any thought of a reconciliation between herself and her
husband soon vanished when Alix realised that Kirby had
chosen her successor . . .

STAY THROUGH THE NIGHT *by Flora Kidd*
Virtually kidnapped aboard Burt Sharaton's yacht, Charlotte
was told that if she didn't co-operate with him, he would ruin
her father . . .

HELL OR HIGH WATER *by Anne Mather*
Jarret Manning was attractive, successful, experienced — and
Helen Chase felt mingled antagonism and fear every time she
met this disturbing man.

CANDLE IN THE WIND *by Sally Wentworth*
Shipwrecked, her memory lost, Sam had to believe her
companion Mike Scott when he told her she was his wife . . .

WHITE FIRE *by Jan MacLean*
Rana had fallen wildly in love with Heath Markland, to the
fury of her domineering mother. But perhaps she knew something about Heath that Rana didn't . . .

A STREAK OF GOLD *by Daphne Clair*
Eight years ago, Ric Burnett had cruelly told Glenna to get
out of his life — but now they had met again . . .

Available January 1980

If you have difficulty is obtaining any of these books from
your local paperback retailer write to:

Mills and Boon Reader Service
P.O. Box No 236, Thornton Road, Croydon, Surrey CR9 3RU.

192